Ghostly Rules

Lorna Shadow cozy ghost mystery - book 6

K.E. O'Connor

K.E. O'Connor Books

Chapter 1

I watched the horses pulling a glass enclosed carriage as they passed the car, dipping my head in respect as they reached my window. Giant black plumes of feathers danced on top of the horses' bridles.

"Are you sure this is the place?" My best friend, Helen Holiday squinted at the open gates of the Nottinghamshire mansion she'd pulled up outside of.

"This is it." I double checked the details the recruitment agency had sent through on my phone. "Creighton Mansion." My gaze shifted to the three sleek, black limousines that followed the carriage. All the mourners were dressed in sombre black, and several women had net veils over their faces and were discreetly wiping their eyes as they passed.

"Did you get a look at who was in the carriage?" Helen craned her neck. "It had better not be our new employer, or we've just wasted half a tank of gas getting here."

"Are you going to ask for that back, or shall I?" I shook my head before turning to stare at the flower covered glossy black coffin with its silver handles, sitting on a carpet of velvet. "I can see the name Lonnie spelt out in flowers."

"That's a relief," she said. "We need to find Elita Cornell, not someone called Lonnie. At least our new jobs are safe."

"I always knew you were the caring type."

"I'm very caring! I care very much about the amount of money we have in our bank accounts. And I care that we can afford to eat every night. And I know Flipper would object if you told him there wasn't enough money for his dog treats."

At the sound of his name, Flipper's gray and white head shot up from the back seat, and he looked at me hopefully. His favorite word was *treat*.

"Don't get any ideas," I said to Flipper. "We've got ages until dinner."

Flipper gave me a slow blink of his ice blue eyes before laying back down and settling his head on his paws. The back seat of the car was his favorite place to be, and Flipper loved nothing more than taking a long nap when Helen was driving.

"Perhaps we should come back later," I said. "If it's a family funeral, there won't be anybody home, and they won't want to deal with us if they're in mourning."

"Give the agency a call and see if they know anything about the funeral," Helen said.

I pulled my phone out again and called Josie at the recruitment agency. Since we'd signed up to the agency, she'd been great at finding us employment with wealthy and upper-class families. I was a whizz as a personal assistant, and Helen was nothing short of a genius when it came to creating new clothing or adapting something to make it the perfect fit. She also did her fair share of the laundry and baking.

My phone connected after the second ring.

"Prestige Recruitment Agency. Josie speaking."

"Josie, it's Lorna Shadow. We've arrived at the Cornell house and discovered everybody leaving for a funeral."

"Oh dear," Josie said, her usually bright sunny voice lowering. "I'd forgotten that was today. I meant to warn you. What bad timing, you getting there as the funeral is about to take place."

"Who died?" I asked. "We saw the name Lonnie."

"That's right. It was Lonnie Cornell," Josie said. "He's your employer's ex-husband. They've been separated for some time. I believe they still lived in the same house."

"That's a bit odd. A divorced couple still living together."

"Apparently, Lonnie loved Creighton Mansion," Josie said. "Have you tried knocking to see if anyone stayed behind to be there when you arrived?"

"Not yet. Are you sure it's not going to bother the family?" I wasn't certain intruding on the Cornells when they were in mourning was appropriate.

"I can't see it being an issue," Josie said. "Elita Cornell mentioned she'd need help with post funeral arrangements. I'm certain you'll be welcome. I hope it's not a problem for you. I know grieving people can be... tricky."

"Nope. It's not a problem for us," I said.

"And this is the perfect fit for you and Helen." Josie's voice warmed as she flipped into her over the top sales mode. "With your old employers heading to Malta for three months, and this job coming in to cover you until they get back, it seemed ideal. Don't let a little funeral get in your way."

"Not to mention that this family is paying double our usual rates." Helen had been listening to the conversation in the seat next to me.

I nodded. When Josie had called to offer Helen and me a three-month stay with the Cornells, I was reluctant. I preferred to work in places for longer than that, get to grips with my job, and make sure everything was running smoothly. Well, whenever the ghosts allowed that to happen.

And that was the trouble. I sometimes got involved in things I shouldn't and ended up losing my job.

Josie had assured me this would be easy, and with the excellent pay offered for Helen and me, I'd decided to take the risk and accept the position as Elita Cornell's personal assistant.

"It won't do any harm if we take a look around," Helen said. "If nobody's about, we can wait in the car until the family gets back."

I jumped at the sound of someone tapping a fingernail on the glass and turned to see a broad shouldered, muscled man in a black suit and wraparound sunglasses peering in at me. "I'd better go," I said to Josie, not taking my eyes off the menacing figure outside the car.

"I'm sure everything will be fine," Josie said. "Let me know if you have any problems. I'm a phone call away. Have a lovely day."

I removed the phone from my ear as the man continued to glower at me.

"Who's that?" Helen stared at the man.

"Not a clue." But the nervous roll of my stomach made me think it was someone I didn't want to get any closer to. "Are you illegally parked?"

"There are no road markings on this country lane," Helen said. "I'm not doing anything wrong."

"He doesn't look like he agrees with that."

Mr. Sunglasses gestured at me to undo the window.

I glanced at Helen. "Maybe we should drive away. He looks shifty to me."

Helen stared at the man. "If he causes any trouble, we can set Flipper on him. And I'm wearing my best stilettos. A quick whack on the head with one of those and he'll be out for the count for hours."

"You'll have to get close to be able to whack him with a shoe," I said. "And have you seen the size of his hands? He could crush you like a paper bag."

Helen leaned over and looked at the man's hands. "Okay, you can attack first and create a distraction. I'll take him from behind."

I wrinkled my nose and then slid down my window and looked at the man. "May we help you?"

"What's your business here?" Mr. Sunglasses asked, his voice a low grumble.

"We're here to see Mrs. Cornell," I said. "Have we come at a bad time?"

"You could say that. I need to see some ID."

I reached for my purse, but Helen grabbed my arm.

"Who are you?" Helen asked Mr. Sunglasses.

"I work for the family." He held out a large, stubby-fingered hand. "Show me some ID or I'll have to move you on."

I pulled out my driver's license and handed it to him. "We're starting work for Mrs. Cornell today."

He looked at my license and then handed it back. "Which one?"

"Which one what?"

"There's more than one Mrs. Cornell living here?"

"Oh! How many are there?"

"There are three in residence," Mr. Sunglasses said, his shoulders slumping.

"Elita," Helen said, flashing him her biggest smile. "Lorna's going to be her personal assistant, and I'm her seamstress. And you are?"

Mr. Sunglasses grunted and remained by the car. I couldn't tell if he was looking at us because of his opaque shades.

"Elita must be attending Lonnie's funeral." I tucked my license back into my purse.

"That's very possible," Mr. Sunglasses said.

He was getting on my nerves. "Is there anywhere we can wait until the family returns?"

For a second, I wondered if I'd spoken a different language, because Mr. Sunglasses seemed frozen to the spot, his arms hanging by his sides and his mouth open.

He gave a quiet grunt and took a step back. "Go through the gates and drive up to the house. Park out front. I'll get someone to show you inside."

I nodded and shut my window as Helen drove toward the gates of Creighton Mansion.

"I hope we won't be seeing much of him," Helen said as she glided the car through the large, ornately carved black gates and along a gravel driveway. "He sucked the joy right out of the air. And did you see how he ignored my best smile?"

"It's hard to believe that someone is immune to your charms."

"I know! I could feel myself getting more miserable every second he was looming over us in that silly suit," Helen said. "And he needs a tailor. The shoulders of his suit were all wrong on him."

"He looked like a nightclub bouncer," I said, "all that menace, muscle, and black clothing. Why do the Cornells need someone like that lurking around outside?"

"He didn't scare me," Helen said. "I bet it's all an act. On the inside, he's as soft as a marshmallow, likes bubble baths and hot chocolate, and has a pet rabbit called Mr. Fluffles."

Helen could be right. Even so, I didn't fancy getting on the wrong side of Mr. Sunglasses.

We pulled up outside the front of a large, white, modern mansion. A set of steps led to black double doors at the front that was flanked by columns. The roof had a wraparound balcony, the edges of which were adorned with carved urns. Everything looked clean, bright, and new.

I spotted giant floppy black ribbons tied around the trees next to the house and an enormous black ribbon on the front door knocker.

I opened the back door of the car, and Flipper jumped out, taking a few seconds to stretch before looking around his new environment.

"It's different from our last house," I said to him. "No cats for you to make friends with. You'll be on your own this time and will have to entertain yourself." Our last employer had kept fifty cats in a sanctuary in the grounds of her estate. Flipper had enjoyed himself as he tried to make friends with as many as possible. The results had been mixed, and he'd ended up with more than a few scratches on his nose as he'd investigated who was a feline friend and who was a foe.

Flipper gave me a doggy smile before trotting away, not seeming to mind the lack of companions, his nose to the ground as he took in the new scents around him.

I looked at my cream sweater covered in small butterfly prints and my blue skirt. I felt inappropriately dressed. Spring pastel colors weren't the right thing to wear in the middle of a family in mourning.

Helen's attire was no better. She was in a light green dress and nude stilettos, and her blonde curls were secured off her face with a giant green butterfly clip. "Let's go inside and see who's about. Maybe we can get someone to show us around while we're waiting."

"I'll get our bags."

Before I'd had a chance to open the trunk of the car, the front door opened and an almost identical version of Mr. Sunglasses emerged. He strode toward us, his arms loose by his sides and a muscle twitching in his jaw.

I resisted the urge to take a step back as he drew nearer.

"Miss Shadow and Miss Holiday." It wasn't a question as he looked at each of us in turn. "You're to come with me."

"And you are?" Helen asked.

The man's head swiveled in her direction. "I'm employed by the Cornells."

"I figured that out for myself," she said. "What's your name?"

The pink tip of the man's tongue showed for a second. "They call me Hog."

I pressed my lips together to stop from laughing. "Is that a nickname?"

"Lonnie gave it to me," Hog said.

"Like a pig?" Helen made a snorting sound and wrinkled her nose.

"Do you have a problem with that?" he asked. His shoulders bunched, and I realized why he'd got the nickname as his neck vanished and his lip curled to reveal porcine-like teeth.

I had to look away and mask my smile. Hog would crush Helen in a second if she kept riling him, but the look of incredulity on her face was too much.

"The name suits you," Helen said, after a few seconds of awkward silence. "You can give us a hand with the bags. A strong swine like you will have no problem with a couple of small cases."

I looked back to see Hog's jaw clench, then he gave a swift nod, grabbed both cases, and stomped into the house without another word.

"It might not be a good idea to annoy the hired muscle," I whispered to Helen as we followed behind Hog at a safe distance.

"I couldn't help it," she said. "What a ridiculous nickname. You think they'd give him a name like Brutus or Spartan. You know, to complement all that pent-up anger and those muscles."

"You've been checking him out?" I grinned. "I didn't know you were into muscles."

"His are hard to miss," Helen said. "He blocks out the sun his shoulders are so broad."

"Wait here." Hog pointed to the bottom of a set of sweeping, curved stairs that led to the first floor, before striding up them. He returned a moment later empty-handed, and I had to hope he hadn't decided to sling our cases out the nearest window in revenge for Helen's teasing.

"This way." Hog gestured for us to follow him along the hallway, which had a cluttered, busy feel to it. The pale-gray carpet felt luxurious under my feet, and there were gaudy, bright pieces of furniture dotted around. Despite the cheery colors, there was something in the house that made me uneasy. It was a feeling of tension as if the whole house was coiled on a spring and about to release at any second. It was just waiting for a trigger.

I glanced around but couldn't see any reason for this feeling. It was different from the sensation I felt whenever a ghost was around. Whatever it was, it set my teeth on edge, and I had to hope it was only temporary. Maybe the funeral had made everyone tense, and I was picking up on those feelings. I could feel my shoulders rising toward my ears as the atmosphere seeped into my pores.

I looked over at Helen to see if it was affecting her, but she seemed her usual cheerful self, and Flipper was happily following along behind us, slowing now and again to sniff an interesting smell or peer into a corner.

Whatever was going on here, only I could sense it, and I didn't like that. It had better not be a portent of things to come.

Chapter 2

Hog had left us alone in one of the ground floor lounges. Everything in this room was white, from the couch to the marble fireplace. And it all looked brand new, so much so, I was reluctant to touch anything in case I made it dirty.

"What's keeping Hog?" Helen asked. "I didn't expect him to stick us in a room and abandon us. He could at least have shown us around or kept us entertained while we waited for the family to get back."

"What would you have him do to amuse us, pig impressions?"

"No! Although that would be fun," Helen said. "He could have told us about the family and if there's anyone we need to be careful of."

"We need to be careful of Hog and that other sunglass wearing goon outside," I said. "Besides, maybe he thinks someone from the family should show us the house." I peered out one of the bay windows and into the back garden.

There was a large swimming pool outside surrounded by a terraced area. Beyond that, a neat lawn and flower beds, full of bright yellow and purple spring colors. The hedges in the distance had been shaped like hares.

"Zach would like it here," I said. "He'd enjoy working in this garden. Although, I bet keeping those animal shaped hedges trimmed is a nuisance."

Zach Booth was my boyfriend and a dab hand when it came to anything horticultural. He'd just finished a year-long job and was spending time putting the finishing touches to our new house. A house I'd be moving into with him, Helen, and Zach's brother, Gunner. It was a daunting prospect, but one tinged with excitement.

"Why don't we take a look around ourselves?" Helen walked to the door and turned the handle. "Hang on a second. Hog has locked us in!"

"It's probably just stuck."

"It's not. It's locked! Anyone would think we can't be trusted."

"You do look kind of shifty," I said.

Helen glared at me. "Aren't you worried that Hog's locked us in here? Why would he do that?"

"I am worried, and I don't know." Right at that second, I was more interested in what I'd seen in the distance. I rubbed my eyes, not certain if what I was seeing was real. "I've just seen a tank."

"What are you talking about?" Helen rattled the door handle again.

"There's a tank in the garden." I squinted and spotted more military vehicles. "And a plane and some sort of missile launcher. And maybe a helicopter, but it's hidden by some trees."

"Someone in the family must be a collector," Helen said. "Don't concern yourself with the antiques in the garden. Get over here and help me with this door before I'm forced to break it down."

"Don't do that. It won't make a good impression on our first day." I took a final look at the weird garden ornaments, walked over and tried the door handle. A sliver of concern shot through me as the door refused to budge. "He must have his reasons for locking us in."

"The reason being he's an idiot." Helen thumped on the door a couple of times.

I checked my watch. We'd been here over an hour. I walked around the room and had a quick look through the desk drawers for any sign of a key, but there was nothing to aid in our escape.

There were dozens of family photos in white frames on top of the desk and mantelpiece. The family shared the same Mediterranean colored skin, dark hair, and dark brown eyes. Not many of them seemed to know how to smile, though.

"I'm going to try a window." Helen strode away from the door toward the bay window. "If Hog won't let us out the door, we can get out this way."

"If we get out, where are we going to go? And why do you want to get out so badly?" I asked. "Unless you're desperate for the bathroom, can't you wait a bit longer?"

"I'm desperate not to be a prisoner." Helen pulled back the bolt on the window. "We work here; we're not slaves. We should be able to come and go as we please." She shoved her shoulder against the window and began to push it up.

An ear-splitting alarm rang through the house, making us both jump.

"You did that," I said to Helen. "Stop messing with the window. You triggered an alarm."

"Why is there an alarm on the window?" She dashed away from the window and stared at it with wide eyes.

The door to the living room opened. Two men wearing black suits and sunglasses charged in. One had his hand inside his jacket as if he was going to pull out a weapon and attack us.

"Is there a problem, ladies?" the taller of the two men asked, his head pivoting around as he surveyed the scene.

"I was trying to get the window open to get some air," Helen stammered. "I didn't realize it would do that."

One of the men hurried to the window, closed it, and shot the bolt back into place. The alarm instantly stopped. "There are a lot of antiques in this house. You can never be too careful. All the downstairs windows have alarms that are triggered unless we turn them off. That way, we know if there are any unwanted intruders attempting to break in and take what isn't theirs."

"We're not unwanted intruders," I said. "But we would like to know why we've been kept in this room and haven't been able to get out."

The two men stood side by side in silence, their hands behind their backs. For all I could see, they might be rolling their eyes at me. Or asleep. I needed to get myself a pair of those sunglasses. They were sort of cool.

I waited for an answer, but the men seemed content to stand there, blocking the doorway.

"Can either of you tell me why we're being kept in this room?" I asked, my patience running out. "Just a clue will do. You can mime it for me if you like."

"Yes! Lorna is great at figuring out mimes, and I'm good at charades," Helen said. "How many syllables are we talking?"

"We're following orders," the shorter man said. "You need to wait here until the family returns."

"Any chance of a bathroom break?" I asked.

"That can be arranged."

"Who set off the alarm?" A shrill female voice sounded from behind the men, and they tensed and turned away.

A bird-thin woman with silver hair in a neat bob and deep laughter lines around her eyes appeared. She sat in a wheelchair, which she pushed forward briskly, her dark brown eyes boring into the two men in front of her.

"Do I have to repeat myself?" she snapped.

"It was an accident," the taller minder said. "The blonde lady tried to open a window without knowing the rules."

The elderly woman peered around the men to where Helen and I stood. Her gaze traveled over both of us in turn. "And you are?"

Even though she was the smallest person in the room, this lady gave off an air of power. It was similar to the strange vibe I got when I'd first entered the house.

I'd have much rather crossed swords with the two muscled sunglass wearing goons than her. "We're starting work with Elita. I'm Lorna Shadow and this is Helen Holiday."

The woman clicked her tongue against her teeth. "And these idiots left you in here on your own?"

"We were told to," the taller minder looked at his colleague, and they shrugged in unison.

"You can both leave." The woman dismissed them with a wave of a bony hand, her sharp gaze remaining on us.

The men left without saying a word and shut the door behind them.

The woman wheeled herself closer. Her fingers were covered in expensive rings embedded with diamonds and emeralds.

"Do you need a hand with your chair?" Helen asked.

The woman snorted. "I've been pushing myself around in this thing for years. I'm not going to start asking for help now. Besides, I have a man who deals with that when I need him."

Helen ducked her head and took a step back. It looked like she was feeling the same vibes as me when it came to the silver-haired firecracker in front of us.

"I'm Sylvia Cornell, your employer's ex-mother-in-law." She grinned. "That's quite a mouthful. You may call me Sylvia."

"We're sorry to turn up at such a sad time," I said. "It must be difficult losing a son."

Sylvia's chin dipped before her stern gaze returned to meet mine. "It's part of life in this family. Loss is to be expected."

I glanced at Helen. Her face looked as puzzled as I felt. "Did you go to the funeral?"

"I stayed for the service," Sylvia said, "but didn't want to hang around with all the sycophants telling me how wonderful Lonnie was. They won't get anything from me by throwing around their smooth lies."

Why would mourners want to feed the deceased's grieving mother lies? I chewed on my bottom lip, not sure how to respond.

"We're going to have a small family wake here," Sylvia said. "The others will return shortly. Elita will be with them. She'll want to meet you both. She's been stressed out over the funeral arrangements."

Flipper loped over from where he'd been investigating the corner of the room and wagged his tail as he stared at Sylvia.

"He's a fine looking fellow." She petted Flipper's head. "Is he yours?"

I nodded. "Flipper's my assistance dog."

"He assists you with your work?" Sylvia gave me a strange look. "What does he do, sniff out overdue bills that need filing?"

I smiled. "Nothing like that. I get fainting episodes from time to time. He alerts me when one's on the way. He's good at picking up when I'm not feeling myself." Well, he alerted me to the presence of ghosts, and they made me feel strange, so it was close enough to the truth.

Sylvia reached around the back of her chair and pulled an oversized black leather purse onto her lap. She unclipped the top, and a small white furry head popped out. "This is Reggie. The two of them can be friends."

The tiny pure white dog hopped out of the purse and sat on Sylvia's lap. He looked about the room before his gaze settled on Flipper and his eyes narrowed.

From that expression, I doubted Reggie was friends with anybody. "I'm sure they'll get along fine. Flipper's an easy-going dog."

"I'm sure he is," Sylvia said. "I can sense that about him. And as for those fainting fits you mentioned, it's most likely because you have the sight."

"I'm sorry?"

"I can see it in you, girl." Sylvia waved a hand at me. "You're one of those psychics."

"I'm not," I said, a stir of unease running through me. Did Sylvia know something about my ghost seeing ability?

"You know things." She gave a confident nod. "And you can stop looking so worried. I'm the same as you. It takes one to know one, especially with our talents."

I glanced at Helen, who gave me a worried look. This conversation had headed into weird territory very quickly. "What's your special talent, Sylvia?"

"I'm sixth sense enhanced," she said. "My mother used to call it a curse. I see it as a blessing. I have an ability most people are too blunt to recognize, or they ignore the signs if they have some latent talent in them. It's too scary for most to open up to. Get past the fear, and it's worth it."

Sylvia's words were unsettling. "I can't predict the future if that's what you mean."

"Well, I can. And I see the two of you doing great things in your short time here. Mark my words, your presence in this house is most welcome and needed. There has been unrest here. That needs to change." Sylvia petted Reggie's head. "I had a vision we'd be visited by two angels who would rescue this family from the dark path being taken and help everyone back to where they should be. And here you are."

"That's flattering," Helen said. "I don't think anybody's ever called me an angel before. Well, only a few guys who had a drink in their hands and too little sense in their heads."

Sylvia laughed. "You're going to fit right in here."

"I'll do a good job while I'm here," I said. "But I'm not sure about rescuing anybody from a dark path. What do you mean? Is your family under some kind of threat?"

Sylvia played with Flipper's ears as he sat happily next to her. Reggie growled quietly, jealousy clear on his fuzzy face. "This family has become... corrupt. We used to have such a true path. We knew what we were doing and how we were going to do it. Ever since Lonnie's last job, everything's gone wrong. I'm surprised he hasn't been shot long before this."

"Someone shot your son?" Helen squeaked.

Sylvia shook her head. "Nothing so dramatic. Although, it has been tried many times. There aren't many Cornells who haven't at least been grazed by a bullet." She rolled up the sleeve of her black dress to reveal a faded pink scar on her forearm.

"You've been shot?" Helen's mouth gaped open. "Why would anyone want to shoot you?"

"I haven't always been a little old lady in a wheelchair." She rolled her sleeve down. "Forty years ago, I'd have given both of you a run for your money, in the fight department and the looks department. I was known for my... ample charms." She looked at her flat chest and gave a shrug.

Helen snapped her mouth shut and looked at me, panic in her eyes.

"Do you mind me asking how your son died?" I was keen to clear up any possibility that a gun had been involved. What was this family into to make people want to shoot them?

"He was electrocuted," Sylvia said. "Silly fool loved to listen to the golden oldies on the radio when he was in the bath, and insisted on using an old-fashioned radio his late father gave him. He used to balance it on the edge of the bath, turn up the volume, and sing along at the top of his voice. I told him it was dangerous, but he didn't listen to me. The radio was plugged into the mains. When it hit the water, that was it. My Lonnie was found dead after the house lights went out. He fried the electrics when he died. How's that for making a grand departure?"

"Well, at least he died doing something he enjoyed," Helen said.

That comment earned her a glare from Sylvia. "Better than being shot in the back of the head, I suppose."

I blinked at that comment. I should have done my research on this family and not taken Josie's word that the job would be an easy one.

"All of that is in Lonnie's past, anyway," Sylvia said. "And, as he got older, he had less to worry about. In fact, that's why he went straight."

Chapter 3

"When you say straight, what do you mean?" I asked Sylvia. She was talking as if her family were right out of the movie *Goodfellas*.

She flapped her bony hands in front of her face. "It's nothing. I shouldn't have mentioned it. Ignatius never likes me to talk about these things with people he doesn't know. It makes him tense."

She definitely should have mentioned it! I opened my mouth to ask more questions, just as the door was shoved open and a dark-haired, tanned man of about thirty strode in.

His chocolate brown eyes narrowed as he spotted Sylvia. "This is where you've been hiding."

Sylvia glanced at the man and sighed. "I haven't been hiding. I've been getting to know our new house guests."

"Ladies." The man glanced at me and Helen. "Sylvia, you promised you'd go straight to your room when we returned. I only brought you back from the service early because you said you weren't feeling well."

She sighed again. "Michael Maccarone, meet Lorna and Helen. Most of his brains are in his overly-developed biceps, and he has yet to learn good manners."

Michael's hands clenched, and he shuffled his feet. "My apologies for not making a formal introduction, but I can't leave you on your own. Elita wouldn't like it."

"Elita knows I can take care of myself." Sylvia smiled and winked at me. "And you don't need to say sorry. We love you just the way you are. Girls, if you ever have a head that needs to be broken, Michael's your man. He's also good at opening stuck jar lids and lifting heavy objects."

A faint blush crossed Michael's cheeks as he took hold of the handles on the back of Sylvia's wheelchair. "It's nice to meet you, ladies. I didn't mean to be rude, but Mrs. Cornell needs her rest, doctor's orders. She shouldn't overexert herself, and she shouldn't push herself around in this chair. That's part of my job."

"Such nonsense," Sylvia said. "The doctor doesn't know what he's talking about. If I don't get any exercise, I'll be too weak to do anything. Now, why don't you be a good boy and get us all some tea and cake? I want to learn more about Helen and Lorna."

"I'll call through to the kitchen and get them to arrange that for you," Michael said.

From the tight set of his shoulders, he was uncomfortable being bossed around by Sylvia. I also got the impression that was how she operated and was used to getting her own way.

The tense feeling I had increased as I heard voices in the hallway. I couldn't shake the bad feeling I had about this family. It might be a good idea to get out while we still could, make some excuse to leave before even starting work.

The menacing feel in the house was growing worse and, along with it, a headache was developing behind my eyes.

Sylvia cocked her head. "That's the rest of the family back from the service. You must come and meet them."

"Perhaps we shouldn't," I said. "A family wake is a private affair. You must want time to grieve. Having two strangers in your midst will make that difficult."

"I insist," Sylvia said. "The family will appreciate having something positive to focus upon. And the two of you brighten up the house. It's been a miserable place with all the backbiting and mean comments people say to each other. We need some fun."

I looked at Helen and gave her a discreet shrug. It appeared we had no choice but to attend the wake and meet our new employer there.

Sylvia spun her chair out of Michael's grip with surprising speed and shoved herself forward.

Michael went to grab the back again, but she shoved one wheel of the chair over his large, black-clad foot and waved him off. "Stop nannying me. I can look after myself."

He shot me an exasperated look, before limping behind the wheelchair at a discreet distance. He must value his toes enough not to risk forcing Sylvia into doing something she didn't want to do.

"Do we have to go to this wake?" Helen looked at her brightly colored dress. "Won't they think it's odd we're there?"

"I would if a couple of strangers rocked up at a family funeral I was attending, but it looks like we aren't getting an option to escape."

We followed Michael and Sylvia and walked the short distance along the hallway into a smart parlor, which was decked out in scarlet and gold furnishings.

In the center of the room sat a large table, covered with a red tablecloth, and groaning under the weight of food and drink.

"Yummy! Look at all the food," Helen said. "Maybe this won't be so bad."

I nodded, but my attention was drawn to an intense conversation taking place by the window.

"It's not right she's here." A slim, dark-haired woman glared at a weeping older woman on the opposite side of the room.

"Lonnie would want her here. She's a part of this family as much as you are." A tall, immaculately dressed man with slicked back hair stood next to the woman.

"I'm his wife!"

"As was she," the man muttered, "until you took him away from her."

"That's not my problem. She should have learned how to keep hold of her man." The woman sniffed and looked around. Her gaze settled on me for a second before shifting away. "I want her gone."

"I'm going nowhere!" The older woman threw down the handkerchief she held and stalked over. "This is my house. You should be the one leaving. You're an embarrassment to this family."

"I'm the embarrassment! You're the one who couldn't keep hold of Lonnie, despite all the filler in your face. And how many facelifts have you had? A dozen wouldn't make any difference. He was always going to be with me."

Sylvia settled back in her wheelchair, a look of grim satisfaction on her face. "They can't stop fighting over my Lonnie, even though he's gone."

"Who are they?" I whispered.

"Elita Cornell, Lonnie's ex-wife, and Chelsea, the new Mrs. Cornell," Michael muttered. "And the guy next to Chelsea is Ignatius Cornell, Lonnie's older brother."

"And the women are as crazy as each other," Sylvia said. "This should be fun."

"You're an absolute cow!" Elita threw the contents of her glass into Chelsea's face.

Chelsea screeched as one of her false eyelashes drifted down her cheek. She thrust her own glass at Ignatius and ran at Elita, her long red nails aimed at her eyes.

Ignatius stepped between them and held them apart before they clashed. "Ladies, now isn't the best time to sort out your differences. Lonnie loved you both in his own way. He made it clear he expected you to get along if you were to stay in this house. I'm sure neither of you wishes to leave."

"She should leave." Chelsea jabbed a finger in the air. "She's past her best. If she was a dog, she'd have been put to sleep by now."

Flipper growled at that comment and lowered his head, causing everyone in the room to look at us.

I waved at all the curious faces, despite my desire to hide under the table. "Hi. Nice to meet you all."

Sylvia cackled out a laugh. "Get used to this. This is what happens every day in this household. It's better you see what things are like straight away. You never know, you might decide it's not the place for you."

That's exactly what I was thinking. The family was crazy, and the house was creepy. I didn't want to be here.

"Who are these women?" Elita asked.

"You hired them." Sylvia wheeled herself toward the food table and piled a plate high with cheese pastries.

Elita glared at Chelsea before shrugging off Ignatius's grip and walking toward us, her gaze running over me and Helen. She was an attractive woman, and from the soft lines around her mouth and eyes, I got the impression she hadn't had a facelift like Chelsea claimed, but simply looked after herself. Her hair was dyed a deep glossy chestnut, and she had a trim figure. The watch on her wrist sparkled with diamonds, matching the jewels around her throat.

"Are you Lorna and Helen?"

I nodded and extended my hand. "Elita Cornell?"

"Yes. I'm glad you were able to find me in all this chaos." Elita waved a hand in the air.

"I know our timing isn't great," I said. "We can come back later."

"No, not at all. I'm sorry you had to see my dispute with Chelsea," Elita said. "She's yet to learn her place in the household. I'm planning to demote her to kitchen hand when I get the chance."

Chelsea snorted, obviously listening into the conversation, before turning her back on us and staring out the window.

"We should leave," Helen said. "We don't want to be in the way."

"There's no need for you to go," Elita said. "And, I hate to say it, but Sylvia has a point. It's often a bit feisty around here. You need to know what you're getting yourselves into. Not every day is like this, but we all have our challenges to face." Her gaze hardened as she looked at Chelsea, who was dabbing drink from her face with a linen napkin.

"Ladies, allow me to introduce myself." A tall, slim man in a charcoal-gray three-piece suit stopped by my side and smiled. "I'm Carson Rosso."

"He was Lonnie's right-hand man," Elita said.

"And now, I'm yours," Carson said smoothly. "That is, if you wish me to remain here."

Elita sighed and brushed a hand down her fitted black dress. "Right now, I'm not sure what I want. Well, I can think of one thing I'd like." Her eyes narrowed as she glared at Chelsea. "But I know she's not going anywhere while there's money to be made around here."

"Why don't you have another drink?" Carson said. "I'll explain things to these lovely young ladies and make sure they understand how the household works." His tone was sickeningly smooth.

A trickle of revulsion slid down my spine at the slimy smile on his face. Here was a man I wouldn't trust as far as I could throw.

Elita turned away. "I could do with something to calm my nerves. I'll catch up with you both later. We can talk about your roles. There's so much to do now that Lonnie's gone. You're both going to be busy."

Carson took hold of my elbow and placed a hand on the small of Helen's back before guiding us away from the rest of the family.

I had to resist the urge to shake his hand off. It felt like a cold hard vice on my flesh.

"As you can imagine, this is a difficult time for the family." Carson released his hold on me. "If you have any questions, please come to me first. I've been with the Cornells for years and will assist you in any way possible."

"I appreciate that," I said. "We weren't aware there had been a death in the family."

"Lonnie's demise was not anticipated."

"I can't imagine anyone's is," Helen said.

Carson shot her a glare. "What I mean is, the family sometimes strolls on the gray side of life. It is a dangerous place to be. Accidents do happen."

"I've never heard of the gray side of life before," I said. "Is that some sort of business you're in?"

"It's the business of discretion," Carson said. "And it's important to remember that if you're joining this family."

"We're just going to be working here. We have no plans to take things any farther than that," I said.

Carson spread his hands wide. "If you're to be a part of the business we run, then you will need to be discreet about everything you see."

"We're discreet." I shot a puzzled look at Helen.

"What is it you do here that needs so much discretion?" Helen asked.

Carson looked around the room, a slow smile spreading across his face. "We keep ourselves safe and make sure to protect our assets."

"I'm guessing that means you don't run a chain of bakeries?" I asked.

Carson's glare turned steely, and I cringed. He looked like an overly-tanned snake about to strike. "Whatever you learn about us, you'll be required to keep the information within these walls. Can I trust you both to do that?"

"We're not going to gossip if that's what you mean," I said. "And we're not new to this kind of work. You only have to check our references to know that."

"Your backgrounds have been thoroughly checked," Carson said. "We did not find anything... unsavory. There was nothing that caused me concern."

I swallowed. That didn't sound like the usual sort of background check we went through when we started a new job. "Neither of us have unsavory backgrounds. We're good at what we do."

"And so are we," Carson said, "but only because the family keeps things to themselves."

"And what if they don't?" Helen asked.

"Then they leave the family," Carson said. The darkness in his gaze lifted, and a false smile spread across his face. "I have a good feeling about the two of you. I'm sure you'll be an asset and help with the smooth running of the estate. Elita's in need of help now Lonnie has gone and has all of this to manage. Don't let her down."

"We never let down our employers," I said. The uneasy sensation I'd experienced since entering the house increased. I couldn't figure out whether it was being so close to the sleazy Carson that was doing it.

Whatever it was, it was time for us to leave. This job might pay well, but everything felt wrong. The atmosphere was so tense I could feel it almost sticking to my skin.

Flipper also seemed to sense something was off and was glued to my side, his anxious gaze flitting from me to Helen as he kept checking to make sure we were okay.

"Enjoy your time here, ladies. If you ever have need of me, I have a private suite in the grounds close to Lonnie's military toys. You're welcome to drop by any time you have a query." Carson gave us a nod before turning and walking back to Elita's side.

I moistened my dry teeth with my tongue and leaned over to Helen. "What do you think of this place?"

"It's super weird," she whispered. "I don't get what all the secrecy's about over the family business. Maybe it's something they're ashamed of, like selling double glazing or one of those scam pyramid schemes you hear so much about."

"That's hardly something to keep so secret, though." I glanced around the room, seeing everyone else engaged in conversation or eating. "I think we should leave."

Helen raised her eyebrows. "Haven't you seen the amazing food on the table?"

"I'm not hungry, and something's wrong here."

"I agree the family is a bit odd, but we've dealt with eccentric before. This isn't so strange. Maybe they don't like outsiders getting involved in a traditional family business and are uncomfortable with us being at the wake. It is making me squirm a bit."

"There's eccentric and then there's dangerous," I said. "Don't you feel the weird vibe in here?"

"A ghost sort of vibe, you mean?"

I shook my head. "Not a ghost. Something darker."

"Are you going to tell me there are demons in this house?" Helen's voice rose in pitch.

I shook my head again. "No, nothing like that. Something is wrong here, and I don't want to find out what it is."

"Can't we just stay for some champagne and canapés?" Helen's bottom lip jutted out. "The food looks good, and it's getting late. We can leave as soon as I've eaten."

I tipped my head back and stared at the ceiling. I was never going to get Helen away until she'd had her fill of tasty treats. "Fine. You stuff your face and get drunk. Then we're getting out of here."

Chapter 4

Half an hour later, Helen had eaten a plate of caviar filled vol-au-vents and drunk two glasses of champagne. She'd just gone to investigate the desserts, giving me a chance to speak to Elita.

"We should go and unpack," I said, "and leave your family to mourn your ex-husband. I am so sorry for our intrusion into something so private."

"You're welcome to stay," Elita said. "We're just getting started. Lonnie loved pretty women at his events, so he'd have liked you and Helen being here."

"We've had a long drive," Helen said as she returned to my side with a plate of mini chocolate eclairs. "It would be nice to have an early night before we get started in our new jobs."

Elita clicked her fingers and beckoned Michael over. "Show the ladies to their rooms."

"Very good," Michael said.

"Don't be long, Michael. I don't like the look in Chelsea's eyes. She's drunk and unhinged and could try to go for me with one of the butter knives." Elita smirked. "Although, I'd like to see her try. I've got a little surprise of my own in my purse in case she gets ideas above her station."

Although I was tempted to ask what the surprise was, I resisted. I looked at Chelsea and noticed the scowl on her face. Fortunately, she was nowhere near any cutlery, so Elita was safe from death by butter knife for now.

Michael nodded and opened the door to the parlor for us. We followed him into the hallway and up the large flight of stairs. Turning right, Michael stopped outside a door and unlocked it.

I poked my head inside and saw a pale pink bedroom; from the carpet to the curtains, everything was a soft shade of pink.

"We have other rooms if this isn't to your liking," Michael said. "The family sleeps in the east wing. The staff have rooms here."

"Where's your room?" Helen asked.

Michael ducked his head. "I'm Elita's bodyguard now. My room is next to hers so I can be on hand in case anybody tries to get into the house without an invitation."

"Why would anybody want to do that?" I asked. "This place has a lot of security. It feels more like a secure unit than a family home."

"It's for protection. The Cornells are well-connected," Michael said. "That means they have enemies. Enemies I intend to put down if they come too close."

I raised my eyebrows and looked at Helen. It was definitely time to get out of here.

Michael left us to investigate our rooms, and I was pleased to see my suitcase had made it up safely. Helen's room was next to mine and was almost the same, apart from the color scheme, which was powder blue and cream.

The second Michael had gone down the stairs, I hurried to Helen's room and shut the door behind me. "We need to escape while we have the chance."

"Escape?" Helen looked at me. "We're not prisoners. Well, other than that first hour when we were locked in a room."

"It feels like we are," I said.

"Is that weird feeling still bothering you?" She did a quick circuit of her room, opening the closet before taking a look in the attached bathroom.

"It is. And it's nothing to do with a ghost. Can't you feel the tension in the air when the family is together?"

"It's hard to miss when Chelsea and Elita are fighting with each other." Helen sat on the bed, and I joined her. "Are you sure you don't want to stay and see how you feel in the morning? It could just be new job nerves."

I tugged on my bottom lip as I considered the question. "The money would be great. What we earn from this job will pay for the furniture in our new house."

"But you don't think it's worth it?"

I looked around the room and imagined living in this house for three months. I found myself grinding my teeth and struggling to breathe. "No. We should leave. And right away. We can sneak out while the family is in the parlor."

"Won't it seem odd the two of us vanishing?"

"The recruitment agency can make our apologies for us. We can say there's been a family emergency or something and we had to leave quickly."

Helen shrugged. "Fair enough. If you can't see yourself working here, then we'll leave."

I hugged Helen, grateful she didn't try to force me to stay. We'd both be out of pocket because of this, and the agency might not be so quick to find us other jobs once we'd let down the Cornells, but I just couldn't stay.

"I'll grab my bag and meet you at the top of the stairs." I left the room and hurried back to my own.

Once inside, I took a moment to tune into whatever weird feeling had me by the throat. It could simply be because the family argued a lot. That was never pleasant to be around.

But maybe it was more than that, and I was picking up on a ghostly presence. If there was one in the house, it wasn't friendly, and I didn't want to meet it.

I looked at Flipper, who was settled on the carpet by the window, his eyes half-closed. Whatever it was, it wasn't something that bothered him, so was unlikely to be ghost related.

I had a freshen up in the bathroom, splashing water on my face and smoothing down my hair, and then picked up my case and headed out of my bedroom with Flipper. I already felt better knowing we'd soon be out of the house.

Helen was waiting for me, and after a check down the stairs to make sure the coast was clear, we crept to the front door.

From the sounds of laughter and music coming from the parlor, it didn't sound like Lonnie's family missed him too much.

I snuck open the front door and ushered Helen and Flipper out, before closing it behind me softly.

Helen pulled up sharply. "Where's the car? I left it right there." She pointed to the gravel driveway, where there was a distinct lack of bright red car.

"Did you leave the keys in it?" It wasn't the first time. "Maybe it got moved."

Helen dug around in her purse and pulled out her car keys. "They're right here. And only you have a key to use the car. Did you give it to someone?"

"Nope. Mine is right here." I dangled my own set of keys in front of her.

"They'd better not have damaged my car by towing it away." Helen's frown deepened as she peered into the gloomy evening.

"Let's check around the side of the house," I said. "We might find it there. I bet it will be just fine."

We carried our cases to avoid making any noise by dragging them across the gravel and ducked as we passed the windows.

Helen rounded the side of the house. "It's not here. What have they done with it? Where's my lovely car?"

I scratched my head as I looked around. "I don't see any sign of a garage, but they must have put it somewhere safe." If we couldn't find the car, we had a big problem. We had no way of getting away from this house and the weird family inside it.

Flipper ran ahead and then returned, before running along the same route again. His tail was up, and he kept looking from side to side as if he heard someone coming.

"Flipper's spotted something," I said. "Since we're not having any luck finding the car, let's follow him and see where he leads us."

Helen nodded, and we hurried after Flipper, who kept glancing over his shoulder to see what we were doing.

There was still no sign of the car, and from the sound of Helen's increasingly loud sighs, she was getting angry about its absence.

Flipper stopped dead and sat down, his ears up and his nose pointed ahead of him.

I looked into the navy-blue gloom around us but couldn't see anything. The night was quiet with barely a breath of wind.

As I continued to stare, a haze appeared in front of me, and I felt a shiver of ice cold run down my back. Something was coming, and it wasn't alive.

The form of a heavyset, dark-haired, middle-aged man appeared in front of me.

Flipper came and sat by my feet. I placed a hand on his head, more to reassure myself than him.

"Who's just joined us?" Helen asked. "You've gone pale. Have we got a new ghost friend present?"

"We do have ghostly company," I said. "And from his coloring and smart suit, I'm guessing it's a family member."

"The recently departed Lonnie?"

The ghost looked at Helen, surprise on his face, and nodded.

"It looks like you're right," I said.

Lonnie started to speak and gestured at us to move away from him, brandishing his hands wildly as he did so.

I glanced over my shoulder, but nobody else was around. "I can't hear you, Lonnie. You're going to have to communicate in a different way. Are you telling us to go away? If you are, don't worry. That's what we're trying to do. We just need to find our missing car."

The ghost frowned and made the same gesture with his hands.

Uneasiness crept through my veins. "I think he wants us to hide."

Lonnie's gaze shot over my shoulder, and he gestured frantically before blinking out of sight.

"What do we need to hide from?" Helen asked.

"Ladies. What are you doing out here?"

Chapter 5

I turned, my teeth gritted, as I spotted the looming bulk of Michael in the shadows. He stepped toward us and folded his arms over his chest.

"We were just..." I was all out of good ideas and looked at Helen for help.

"Well, why are you out here so late?" Michael's gaze flew from me to Helen.

"We wanted to get some air before bed." Helen flashed him her brightest smile.

He appeared unimpressed by that lie. "With your suitcases?"

"We were planning on storing them in the trunk of the car," I said. "Get them out of the way. But we've been having trouble finding it. Do you know where Helen's car is?"

"There's plenty of storage inside." Michael picked up the cases, ignoring my question about the car.

I could see he was testing the weight of them in his hands. It looked like we'd been rumbled.

"We can manage our cases." I tried to take mine, but he didn't acknowledge me.

"I'll take you back to your rooms." Michael turned and walked toward the front door of the house.

"What shall we do?" I asked Helen.

"Follow him. They've got our car and our clothes. And my favorite little red dress is in that case. I'm not leaving without it."

I frowned, not liking the thought of having to go back into the house. "I guess we're spending the night. First thing in the morning, we need to find a way out of here."

As we walked through the front doorway, Sylvia was wheeling herself out of the parlor. She stopped and stared at us. "What's going on here?"

"Miss Shadow and Miss Holiday were getting some... air," Michael said. "They're back now. They won't be going out again after dark."

Sylvia's dark eyes narrowed, and she let out a cackle of laughter. "We can be a bit scary, but there's no need to flee in the night. So long as you follow the rules, you're safe here."

"Are there many rules we need to know about?" Helen asked.

Sylvia cackled again. "I thought you girls were made of sterner stuff than this. Never expected you to run away. I was just telling Lonnie so, when he vanished on me."

Michael shook his head. "Sylvia, Lonnie's not here. You can't tell him anything."

I shot Sylvia a quizzical look. It wasn't so strange for people to talk to those who'd recently died. From her tone of voice, she sounded convinced she'd been speaking to Lonnie in person and not in her head. She'd also mentioned she had a sixth sense. Did that stretch to talking to the dead?

"We weren't running away," Helen said. "But I do want to know where my car is."

"I've taken it to be serviced," Michael said as he stood in the hallway, our cases still in his hands.

"It doesn't need a service," Helen said. "It's running just fine. I look after my car."

"Boss's orders," Michael said.

"I'm the boss when it comes to that car." Helen jammed her hands on her hips. "And I say it's fine as it is. I want it back where I parked it right away."

Sylvia laughed. "There you are! I knew it. You girls aren't frightened of some big men in suits who have forgotten how to smile. Stay! You might find you enjoy it here when you get used to us. It's an entertaining place to be, and there's always some argument or other to referee over." She gestured behind her, where raised voices could be heard. It sounded like Chelsea and Elita were at each other's throats again.

"We would like to know where the car is," I said.

"Like Michael said, it's being looked after," Sylvia said. "We take care of our own. It won't cost you a thing, and your car will purr like a kitten when it's been serviced. Trust us."

I wouldn't be doing that anytime soon. "We can talk about it in the morning."

Sylvia grinned. "Meet me for breakfast. I can let you in on all the family secrets."

Michael cleared his throat. "I believe Elita wishes to spend some time with the ladies tomorrow morning."

Carson walked out of the parlor and stopped when he saw us all in the hallway. "What's going on here? Not having a little party without me?"

"We've given these lovely girls a scare," Sylvia said. "Everything's sorted now."

Carson's eyes narrowed, and he walked closer to me. "What's the problem?"

"There's no problem." I resisted the urge to take a step away. The menace radiating from him made my skin itch.

"I thought we had an understanding," Carson said. "You do a good job here, keep your mouths shut, and you'll be rewarded."

"Actually, we're thinking this isn't the right place for us," Helen said. "And we don't like being told to shut up."

"I never told you to do that." Carson's steely gaze switched to Helen. "I simply advised you that it's wise to be discreet. People who misbehave aren't tolerated in this family."

"Then it's fortunate we aren't family," I said. "We work for you, but that's it."

"It makes you honorary members of our family," Carson said.

Sylvia tutted. "Stuff and nonsense. Carson, you're as much of an employee as these girls. Stop doing your best gorilla impression and trying to intimidate them. They see beyond your bluster and know what a big teddy bear you are when you're not strutting around trying to lay claim to everything."

Carson flashed Sylvia a thin smile. "Lonnie considered me a brother."

"He might have done." Sylvia tapped her fingers on the wheels of her chair. "But he's gone now."

"And that's something we all feel deeply." Carson dipped his head. "But it's important we stick to the rules and don't go changing things. It's worked well in the past. We can't start messing with what works."

"We won't mess with anything," I said. "But Helen's right. This isn't the place for us. You can find people better suited for these jobs." People who didn't mind being intimidated and trapped in a house against their will.

"Don't be hasty in making a decision," Sylvia said. "Take your time in getting to know us. We aren't all as stuck in our ways as Carson."

Carson bowed and took a step back. "I only wish to maintain the family status, keep everything as it should be."

Sylvia raised a hand. "Enough of these boring rules and business talk. I need some air."

Michael took a step forward, but Sylvia waved him away.

"I want these girls to take me outside," she said. "Since they seem to like being outdoors so much, they won't mind pushing a little old lady around the grounds." She gave me an obvious wink.

"You're not supposed to be left on your own," Michael said.

"I won't be on my own. I'll be with Helen and Lorna," Sylvia said. "They know how to take care of themselves. I'm sure they won't mind keeping an eye on me. I can't get up to any mischief while I'm in the garden."

From the twinkle in her eye, I got the impression she could. "We'll be happy to take you." I walked to the back of her chair.

"At least allow me to accompany you," Carson said. "You don't want to burden the girls with your chair."

"You're needed here," Sylvia said, not bothering to look at Carson. "Keep an eye on the rest of the family, since you enjoy doing that so much."

Carson frowned but then nodded and turned toward the parlor.

"I can push the wheelchair," Michael said. "I want to help."

"There's no need. We'll be fine," Sylvia said, her tone softer. "And it sounds as if you're needed as well. Elita and Chelsea can't stay civil when they're sharing the same space. I wonder what Lonnie was doing giving them half the house each in his will. It's as if he wanted to see two women fight to the death over him."

Michael's gaze shot toward the parlor, where the sounds of increasingly screechy insults were being traded.

"You go," Sylvia said to Michael. "I'm in need of some girl time." She gestured at me to get the chair moving.

I obliged, pushing her toward the front door and outside. Helen and Flipper followed me, and I was glad when Helen shut the door, muffling the argument. As we moved away from the house, the tension in my shoulders eased.

"Don't mind Michael being overprotective of me," Sylvia said. "He worries too much. I've known him since he was young and consider him to be a surrogate grandchild."

"He's not the only one keen to keep an eye on you," I said. "Why doesn't your family want you to be on your own?"

Sylvia laughed and pointed ahead of her. "Head to those trees. You can see the city lights at night from there."

I noticed she'd avoided my question. "How long has the family lived in this house?"

"Ever since Lonnie decided we needed to show a united front and stop breaking the law."

I raised my eyebrows and looked at Helen. "What law did he break?"

Sylvia cackled out a laugh. "We're a famous family. It wouldn't be hard to find out. Although, we're not famous in the way you might think."

"Are you more notorious than famous?" Helen asked.

"Clever girl," Sylvia said. "Although we now live in leafy, middle-class suburbia, we're originally from the East End of London. The Cornells used to be close to the Reitz family. Ever heard of them?"

"The gangsters!" This was getting worse.

"That's right," Sylvia said. "I even named my dog after one of the sons. Reggie Reitz was such a smooth talking guy. He even flirted with me, and I was old enough to be his very inappropriate cougar."

"You made your money committing crime?" Helen asked.

She was silent for a long time. "The family never took from people who couldn't afford it."

"Like Robin Hood," I said, not able to keep the sarcasm from my voice.

"Just like him," Sylvia said. "And that's enough of your tartness. We did what we had to. But things changed when Lonnie decided to go straight. He planned one final job before he retired. That was when the trouble began, and it's how we ended up here. I miss London life, but hearing the birds sing in the morning isn't so terrible."

"What was his last job?" Helen asked.

"No, wait!" I said. "We only want to know if it doesn't get us in trouble with Carson. The way he was glaring at me, I wouldn't put it past him to place a horse's head in my bed as a warning to behave."

Sylvia hooted with laughter. "You're thinking of the wrong family. And Carson's not part of this family, no matter how hard he tries. He's a Rosso. They've always worked for us, always have and always will. He's as mean as a stepped on king cobra, though. Stay out of his way and you'll be fine."

That was something I had every intention of doing. "So, what crime did Lonnie commit?"

"This hasn't been proven," Sylvia said as she gestured for me to stop pushing the wheelchair. "If you go blabbing to the authorities about this, I'll deny everything."

I glanced at Helen. "Okay. What happened?"

"The police believe he stole twenty-five million in gold."

"Wow! That's a lot of gold."

"It is. Which makes it hard to move and sell on," Sylvia said. "And where would you hide so much gold? That's the question everyone wants answered. Have you ever held a gold bar?"

"It's on my list of things to do before I die," I said.

Sylvia tutted. "They're heavy. You could only manage to carry a few."

"The gold paid for your move to this house?" Helen asked.

"Not a single gold shaving paid for any of this," Sylvia said. "We've always had money, so we used that to get away, settle down, and find some peace. Have a happy ending."

"But it didn't end well for Lonnie," I said. "Dying in the bath like that is a tragedy."

"It would be if his death was an accident," Sylvia said. "But my Lonnie's still around. And I know why. It was because he was murdered."

I sucked in a breath. "Do you have proof of that?"

"The proof of my own eyes," Sylvia said.

"You saw someone kill Lonnie?" Helen asked.

"No, daft girl," Sylvia said. "Lonnie's still here. Still in the house. I see him, and he's been showing me what happened."

"You can see your dead son's ghost?" I asked.

"Absolutely," Sylvia said, "and he's here for a reason. That reason being he wants to ensure whoever murdered him is put behind bars. Well, receives some sort of punishment. We handle things our own way when it comes to family being killed."

I rubbed my forehead, not sure which bit of Sylvia's revelation to pull apart first. She believed she could see Lonnie's ghost and that he'd been murdered. I ignored the fact she'd hinted the family would do something unpleasant to whoever might have killed him. Oh, and not forgetting the fact Lonnie supposedly stole a load of gold and got away with it.

I decided on a gentle approach with Sylvia. She was old and could be confused. "People often believe they can feel loved ones who've recently died. Is that what you're sensing with your son?"

"Stuff and nonsense," Sylvia said, "and you know it. I see him with my own eyes. My eyesight has always been excellent. Lonnie's here. I saw him the first night after he died. He popped into my bedroom and gave me a fright. Ever since then, he's been hovering around, making a nuisance of himself. He keeps drifting about and making the rooms cold. Don't tell me you haven't noticed him?"

I opened my mouth, but nothing came out.

"Grief makes people experience all sorts of things," Helen said.

"Stop trying to convince me that what I'm seeing isn't true," Sylvia said. "Lonnie is here. He's not going to rest until his murder has been solved."

"And how are you going to solve it?" I asked.

A sly smile spread over Sylvia's face. "I thought you girls might like to help me with that little matter. I get the impression this isn't the first time you've seen a ghost."

"I've never seen a ghost," Helen said. She looked at me with wide eyes.

"What about you, Lorna?" Sylvia asked coyly. "How are your ghost seeing abilities?"

I squirmed under Sylvia's intense gaze. "It's... complicated."

"There's nothing complicated about it," she said. "Don't lie to me, girl. You see ghosts."

Chapter 6

I woke in a tangle of bedsheets, having spent a restless night dreaming about Carson sneaking into the room with a severed horse's head tucked under one arm.

As I blinked my eyes open, I saw Helen's bare feet by my face, her toenails painted a coral pink. Flipper was laying alongside me, stretched out and snoring.

After our bizarre conversation with Sylvia last night, we'd decided the safest thing to do was share a bed. I'd gone top to tail with Helen, Flipper wedged in between us. It wasn't the most comfortable night's sleep I'd ever had, but I was glad of the company.

Helen woke with a start before shuffling around in the bed until she faced me. "Please tell me last night was a horrible dream? Sylvia doesn't want us to investigate a family of criminals and find out which one killed Lonnie?"

"It's all true." I groaned. "I still can't believe what she told us. I've never met anybody else who can see ghosts."

"You're focusing on her ghost seeing talent?" Helen smoothed down her bed messy blonde hair. "What about the killer in the family or the missing gold? All important things."

"It's important to me."

"Are you sure she can see ghosts?" Helen asked. "Sylvia comes across as a bit... eccentric. Maybe she thinks she can see something, but there's nothing there. It could be in her imagination."

"It'll be easy enough to test if Sylvia can really see Lonnie," I said.

"Yes! The next time he appears, we get him to talk to Sylvia and see how she reacts," Helen said.

"It would be sort of amazing if she can see him," I said. It would be great to talk to someone about my ability and not have them think I was losing my mind. "I think it's still time for us to leave. If Sylvia can see Lonnie and doesn't need our help in communicating with him, there's no reason to stay. He can let her know who killed him, and the family will deal with it in whatever gruesome manner they want to. We don't need to be around for that."

"Even though Sylvia asked for our help?"

"She's a warrior trapped in an old lady's body," I said. "You've seen how everyone backs down when she's around. She doesn't need us."

"I'm still okay with leaving if you want to," Helen said. "I'll have a quick shower while you call the agency and get us out of here."

I nodded as Helen left the room before picking up my phone and calling Josie.

"Prestige Recruitment Agency," a voice I didn't recognize said.

"Is Josie there?" I asked. "It's Lorna Shadow, one of her clients. I need to talk to her about my recent work placement. It's not working out the way I'd hoped."

"Josie's on holiday for the next two weeks," the woman on the other end of the phone said. "I can get her to call you when she returns."

"Two whole weeks!" I looked around the bedroom and let out a shaky breath. I didn't think I could survive two more minutes here. "Is there anyone else who can help?"

"Josie likes to handle all of her clients herself." The woman's tone was hesitant. "I'm Cassandra. I work with Josie."

"Please help me, Cassandra." There was no way I could wait until Josie got back from her fun in the sun. "I'm sure Josie won't mind."

"Let me pull up your information and see if I can assist," she said. "We don't like people to be unhappy. Where have you been positioned?"

"With the Cornells," I said. "I'm not sure the work they want us to do is suitable." Even though I hadn't done any actual work for them, the threats from Carson, the tense house atmosphere, and the revelation about a pile of stolen gold was enough to put me off.

I heard shuffling and fingers tapping on a keyboard. "Oh! The Cornells are new clients at the agency. They've paid in advance and well above our usual rates to get someone good. Are you sure you can't manage the work there?"

"I can manage the paperwork just fine," I said. "But the family is... strange." What else could I say? Wanted criminals, sleazy villains with an attitude, light-fingered when it came to other people's cars?

"We would lose any commission if you leave so soon," Cassandra said.

"You can take a cut from all future jobs I do with you." I didn't mind paying so long as we got out of here.

"I see from your work record that you were employed by the Marquis of Hedgeshire," Cassandra said. "Isn't he the chap who keeps pigs in his house?"

I tipped my head back against the wall. "That was a strange hobby of his. The pigs weren't free roaming. They kept to their own part of the house. It was very hygienic." In fact, I got to like the pigs. They used to make cute snorting noises when they wanted a head rub.

"If you can handle the Marquis's eccentricities, you can deal with the oddities of this new family," Cassandra said. "What is it that's making you uncomfortable? I can speak to your new employer, make sure to iron out any concerns so you can stay."

"No! You don't need to speak to them." I didn't want word getting back to anyone in the family that we were concerned. They might consider we were being disloyal and get the thumb screws out.

"Try it for a week and see how you get on," Cassandra said. "I'm sure, once you've settled in, you'll love it. Any serious problems, Josie is back in two weeks. She'll be more than happy to help."

I said a grudging goodbye. The agency wasn't going to be any help when it came to this job. I could tell from Cassandra's tone that they valued the fat commission the Cornells had paid over our safety.

Helen came back into the bedroom, her hair wrapped in a large towel and her fluffy pink dressing gown on. "Any joy with the agency? Are we getting out of here?"

"Not yet," I said. "Josie's on holiday. The woman I spoke to simply told me to suck it up and get on with it."

Helen let out a sigh as she sat on the bed. "What do we do? Sylvia was insistent we assist with finding out who killed Lonnie."

"It's nothing we wouldn't have done ourselves if Lonnie had come to us and asked for help," I said. "And the fact he's still around suggests his death wasn't an accident."

"We'll be investigating a family of criminals," Helen said. "I'm all for helping a ghost in need, but that's reckless."

"Sylvia's got our backs," I said, resigning myself to having to serve time with the Cornells. "She can keep control of Carson and the other goons loitering around the estate."

"Carson gives me the chills," Helen said. "He's got those cold, emotionless eyes you see on serial killers."

"Can't say I've met a serial killer," I said. "You're right, though. We need to keep out of Carson's way."

"I'm happy to oblige with that," Helen said.

I jumped as the phone in my hand rang, then relaxed when I saw the caller was Zach.

"Good morning, beautiful," he said. "How's your new job going?"

"It's been uneventful so far." I didn't want to tell him too much. I knew how alarmed Zach got every time I became embroiled in another ghost mystery. And this one had an added twist to it. "How's the house?"

"It's almost there," Zach said. "The heating is in, and the windows got finished yesterday. Everything is watertight and warm. I'm running the system now and testing it. We'll soon be able to spend the night here."

"That's great," I said, my thoughts still on what to do about the Cornells.

"It is," Zach said, after a short pause. "But I'm not sensing much enthusiasm. Is anything wrong?"

"Not with our new house," I said. "I'm excited it's almost ready to move into. It'll be nice to have a permanent base for everybody."

"It will," Zach said. "You must come take a look. You and Helen will be impressed with how much progress Gunner and I have made."

I bit my lip. Gunner and his insider police knowledge would come in handy right about now. "Is Gunner back at work?"

"Yes. He's used all his leave helping me," Zach said. "He's still coming by on weekends and whenever he's got a day off because of his shift patterns. Do you want to talk to him?"

"I need a favor from him," I said. "Can you ask him to do a background check on the family we're working for?" Gunner could find out more about the Cornells and their dubious past. And he'd be able to advise us if we needed to get out of the house before being enslaved into a life of crime.

"I'm sure he can," Zach said. "Why do you need a background check on them?"

"There's something not right," I said, not willing to reveal the hardcore criminal nature of the Cornells. Zach would freak out, and we weren't at that stage yet. Although, I wasn't far off. "Gunner will have inside knowledge about their past."

"By past, you mean checking to see if they have a criminal history," Zach said. "Exactly who are you working for?"

"They're called the Cornells," I said. "And we turned up on the day of Lonnie Cornell's funeral. He was electrocuted in the bath."

"By accident?"

"Possibly not," I said.

"Is his ghost bothering you?"

"Not so much bothering," I said, "but Lonnie is around. And the family is on the strange side. Lots of burly bouncer types and men in wraparound sunglasses."

"I don't like the sound of this," he said. "You should leave. This family could be dangerous."

"They've not done anything bad to us."

"They stole my car." Helen muttered as she toweled her hair dry.

I shook my head at her and pressed a finger to my lips. Our concerns could be for nothing. Sylvia could be right and the family had turned over a new leaf and weren't involved in anything criminal. But the fact Lonnie was implicated in an enormous gold heist and was dead, suggested otherwise.

"Do you want me to come over?" Zach asked.

"No, you need to stay on top of things at our house."

"Not if you're in danger," Zach said. "I can leave here and get you both out."

"There's no need," I said. "We can look after ourselves. And the money from this job is needed to furnish the house."

"If we survive long enough to pick out our new sofas and beds," Helen whispered.

I glared at her. She wasn't being helpful.

"So long as you're both okay. Any other names you want me to pass onto Gunner?" Zach asked. "I've got Lonnie Cornell here."

"Look into Carson Rosso as well," I said. "He's not family, but he works for them. He likes to throw his weight about."

"Let me know if he's being a problem," Zach said, his tone dark. "I don't care how tough he thinks he is, no one intimidates you and gets away with it."

I felt myself melt as Zach came over all protective. "He doesn't scare me. The scariest person in the family is the old lady. She rules over everything, but I'm not worried about her. She's taken a shine to me and Helen. We'll be alright so long as we keep on her good side."

"What's her name?" Zach asked.

"Sylvia. Are you going to get a background check on her as well?"

"Why not?" he said. "She could be the head of this gang of thugs, and you might be sharing a house with a ruthless killer."

I laughed. "A gust of wind would blow Sylvia over. She's tiny."

"That doesn't mean she isn't lethal," Zach said. "I'll see what Gunner can get on her as well. We don't have to wait for any information he can find. I don't want you in harm's way."

"We'll be fine," I said. "I've got Helen and Flipper with me. And Sylvia likes us. Any trouble, we'll go straight to her and hide behind her wheelchair."

"I still think I should come and get you out of there," Zach said.

I had to admit, I was tempted by the offer. I'd only been awake for a few minutes, and the house's strange atmosphere was already getting under my skin.

Flipper jumped up and stared across the room, a low grumble coming out of him. Lonnie appeared at the foot of the bed and shook his head at me.

I ignored Lonnie for a second. "Helen, what do you think? Should we cut our losses now before things get worse?"

Lonnie clasped his hands together in a begging position and dropped to his knees.

"I'm not the one getting strange feelings about this place," Helen said. "Although, I must admit, the grumpy bouncer types don't make it a comfortable place to work. If you want to go, then we go."

Lonnie floated toward me, still on his knees and his hands clasped in front of him.

I closed my eyes, trying to resist feeling guilty under his pitiful stare. I wanted out of this house but was torn between helping Lonnie and giving myself an easy life.

"Lorna," Zach said. "Are you still there? What do you want to do?"

I took a deep breath and opened my eyes, seeing Lonnie still on his knees. "We'll stay for now. I'll get in touch if we need you to come in and rescue us."

"Make sure you do," Zach said. "Don't go playing the hero. I'm not building this house so I can live in it on my own. I want you here, safe with me and Jessie."

"I know that," I said. "However, if anything happens to me, you'll still have Gunner, Helen, and the dogs to keep you company."

"Don't even joke about something like that," Zach grumbled.

We said our goodbyes, and I shut off the phone.

"It sounds like we're staying," Helen said.

I looked at Lonnie and gestured for him to get off his knees. "For now. But I'm not going to be intimidated by a house full of thugs. We'll do our jobs and keep our heads down."

"What about Lonnie?" Helen asked. "He's not going to leave you alone until you figure out what happened to him."

I let out a sigh as I looked at the ghost. "We'll just have to find out what happened to him quickly. And make sure we're discreet about it."

Chapter 7

Despite feeling uncertain about working for the Cornells, the day had been surprisingly normal. Elita had set me up in a smart study with the latest technology and given me a long list of tasks relating to Lonnie's funeral to deal with. Most of it was writing thank you notes or responding to emails about Lonnie's death. There were also handwritten letters to type up and send out, and Elita wanted research done to see if it was legal to put a person's ashes inside a firework and explode it in public.

That would be a sight to see if she did that to Lonnie's remains.

Lonnie had kept me company on and off for most of the day, drifting around the study as if he had nothing better to do. Maybe he didn't. I had no clue if there was much of a party to be had in the afterlife.

I was finishing up my first day of work and already feeling better about the decision to stay, when Carson strode into the study. My relaxed mood faded as I saw the cold expression on his face.

"I was looking for Elita," he said by way of introduction.

"I haven't seen her all day," I said. "She had some personal matters to attend to."

"She's not in the house?" Carson looked around as if he expected to find her hiding behind one of the sofas.

"Not that I'm aware of." I continued to file away paperwork.

He took a step closer and rested his hands on the desk, his knuckles cracking as he did so. "Where is she?"

I turned away from the filing cabinet. "She must have gone out."

"I've looked everywhere."

I refused to be bullied by Carson. "Like I said, maybe she's not in the house."

"Elita shouldn't be going out on social visits. It's too soon after Lonnie's death."

"I imagine she can do what she wants. She's a single lady."

Carson's knuckles went white as he pressed his hands down on the desk. "Do you have access to her personal diary?"

I bit my tongue and shook my head. Elita had given me the password to her electronic diary that morning and asked me to update some social engagements, but there was no way I would give Carson that information. He had no right to pry into her personal business.

He stood up straight and adjusted his red tie. "Tell Elita to come find me when she returns. There are family matters I need to discuss with her." He didn't wait for my response, and simply strode out of the study.

I looked over at Lonnie, who'd watched Carson with interest as he'd spoken to me. "I'm guessing you didn't employ him because of his social graces."

Lonnie smirked and then shrugged.

"I imagine his skills lie elsewhere." I hadn't failed to notice the bulge in Carson's jacket. Guns weren't a common sight in this country, but I was certain I'd caught a glimpse of some sort of holster.

Lonnie did a few boxing moves around the room.

"Maybe it's time Carson wasn't here anymore," I said to Lonnie. "Since your mom believes you'd gone straight before you died, do you need him around? He could cause trouble and make people think you're still living the high life thanks to crime."

Lonnie frowned and flexed his biceps.

"Michael strikes me as more of the protective type, not Carson. Carson's the mean and evil sort. That's exactly who you don't want hanging around your family."

The study door banged open. Chelsea walked in, her black patent heels clicking on the wooden flooring as she strode to the desk. "What have you been doing for that old hag, Elita?"

I blinked a couple of times. Carson wasn't the only one who needed to learn some manners. "Mainly dealing with matters to do with Lonnie's funeral."

Her red painted lips pinched together. "I should be in charge of that. I'm his wife. Elita's the... cast-off."

"I don't think Elita meant any harm by asking me to handle the paperwork," I said. "I can talk you through what I've done if that would help. It's hard losing a husband. Maybe Elita thought she was helping you during a difficult time."

"She'd never help me." Chelsea flicked through a pile of letters on the desk. "And Lonnie left her to be with me."

"I can show you the thank you notes, and make sure you think the wording is appropriate. You'll know what Lonnie liked better than anyone else."

"All that stuff is pointless," Chelsea said. "I'm not interested in that. What about Lonnie's private papers? What's Elita got you doing with those?"

"Nothing yet." I glanced over at the filing cabinet. I'd seen several large files with Lonnie's name on them. "Is there anything in particular you're interested in?"

"No. I understand Lonnie's business." Chelsea pushed her large, possibly surgically enhanced chest out. "He didn't hide anything from me."

Lonnie flapped his hands in the air and shook his head. It looked like that wasn't true.

"If there's anything you need me to get out of the filing cabinet, just ask," I said. "I'll be happy to help."

"I don't suppose you've noticed anything about his gold?" Chelsea traced a nail backward and forward across the desk, keeping her gaze lowered.

Lonnie shot to Chelsea's side and glared at her.

She shivered and took a step away from the desk.

"His gold?" I decided now wasn't the time to reveal what Sylvia had disclosed about Lonnie's gold heist. "Did he leave you gold jewelry in his will?"

"He gave me all the jewelry I ever wanted while he was alive," Chelsea said. "Lonnie was a generous man."

"What kind of gold are we talking about?"

"Oh! It's nothing." Chelsea's gaze met mine. "Lonnie might have stashed something away. I'd like to know where it is. Let me know if you see anything about his hidden gold stash. The family is being secretive about it. I want my fair share. It's only right, what with me being his wife."

Lonnie shook his head and folded his arms across his chest, his angry glare still fixed on Chelsea.

Chelsea glanced over her shoulder and then leaned closer to me. "If you find anything of interest about

Lonnie's gold, make sure to let me know first." She pulled a bundle of notes from her ample cleavage and passed them to me. "Anything at all. If you do, I'll make sure you get more of that."

I stared at the warm bundle of notes in my hand. "I'm happy to share any information I can with you."

Chelsea tapped the side of her nose and winked at me. "Do that. If you can figure out this mystery, I might employ you as *my* personal assistant. You can get away from Elita and her boring plans. You'll have much more fun in my company. I'm planning a trip to Aspen, and then there's Ibiza to look forward to. Stay on my good side and you can enjoy all of that."

It sounded like my idea of hell. I held out the money. "You don't need to pay me to do this."

Chelsea shook her head and backed away from the desk, not taking the money from me. "Call it a little bonus for future services rendered. And just remember, there's plenty more where that came from." She turned and vanished out of the study while I was still staring at the bundle of money.

Lonnie knocked some pens off the desk, drawing my attention back to him.

"Is Chelsea always like that?" I asked.

He grimaced and nodded.

"Your wife just bribed me to act as her informant against your family. Have you been keeping a secret from her?"

Lonnie adjusted the cuffs on his shirt. He looked at the large gold ring on his wedding ring finger and made a show of removing it.

"She wasn't the wife you hoped she'd be?"

He gave a shrug, his shoulders slumping forward. He drifted over to some photographs on the mantelpiece and pointed at one of Elita surrounded by other family members.

I peered at the picture. They looked happy. It was one of the rare pictures of them where everyone was smiling. Lonnie had his arm draped over Elita's shoulders as she gazed up at him, the love in her expression clear.

"Maybe you're regretting trading Elita in for a younger model," I said. "One who's more interested in this mysterious gold than you?"

Lonnie tugged on his bottom lip and then nodded. He gestured at my chest.

I looked at my tailored pale green jacket. "What are you pointing at?"

He jabbed his finger at me again and mimed holding two breasts on his own chest. He turned around and wiggled his butt at me.

I resisted the urge to roll my eyes. Men, sometimes they were too simple for their own good. "You traded Elita in for someone with bigger boobs and a sexy wiggle?"

Lonnie turned back toward me and hung his head.

"You're right to be ashamed of yourself," I said. "Those things fade and sag. A perky twenty-year-old butt isn't going to look the same on a sixty-year-old."

Lonnie raised his hands in supplication.

I tapped my finger against my lips. "If Chelsea figured out you were only interested in her physical assets and she discovered you had your own hidden assets in the form of gold, it would give her an excellent motive for killing you. With you out the way, she could get her hands on everything."

Lonnie's gaze shifted to the door Chelsea had strutted through, and he nodded.

"You don't remember seeing her in the bathroom just before you died?"

He shook his head and closed his eyes.

"Were you asleep in the bath?"

Lonnie shook his head but kept his eyes closed.

"You had your eyes closed when your killer tossed the radio into the water?"

He nodded and opened his eyes.

"It's a horrible way to die," I said. "If Chelsea was involved, we'll figure out how to prove it. If she keeps chasing after this hidden gold, she's going to make herself the key suspect in your murder."

The door to the study slammed open for the second time. Elita stormed in, followed by a worried looking Helen, carrying a red and black dress and a sewing kit.

"Is everything okay, Mrs. Cornell?" I asked.

She slammed her hand on the desk. "No, it's not. What's that scheming bitch been up to?"

Chapter 8

Slipping the money Chelsea had given me under a pile of paperwork, I pasted a smile on my face. "I'm not sure who you mean."

"I saw Chelsea leaving this office." Elita's kohl rimmed eyes narrowed. "She's always poking her nose into business that doesn't concern her. What did she want?"

I wasn't sure whether to mention her interest in the gold. "She didn't stay for long. She asked about the post funeral arrangements and Lonnie's business."

Lonnie drifted over to the desk, watching Elita as he did so.

Elita shook her head. "Now the hard work's over, Chelsea wants to reap the rewards. It's not going to happen. Whatever she told you to do, don't do it. You're my employee, not hers."

"I understand that," I said. "You have nothing to worry about."

Elita waved a hand at me. "She wants me out of this house. It's never going to happen. Lonnie promised me a place here for as long as I wanted it. That's why he left me half the house in his will. I was his first love, just as he was mine. That little money grubber has come in here and thinks she can take everything away."

"Shall I continue altering your dress?" Helen asked quietly.

Elita's gaze snapped to her, and she nodded. "Yes! Sorry, Helen, I didn't mean to abandon our dress making session. I had to make sure Chelsea wasn't getting her claws into Lorna."

Helen knelt next to Elita and began pinning the hem on her dress, shooting me a grimace as she did so.

"They've only been married for eight months," Elita said. "Chelsea can't own everything after being his wife for such a short time. We were married for fifteen years. I gave Lonnie the best years of my life. I stood by his side, no matter what he did. And he spent time in jail. Did you know that?"

"No." Although the news didn't come as a huge surprise.

"It was nothing serious. The police could never get anything to stick on him. My Lonnie was such a clever man. I waited six months for him to come out, and I visited every single week. I always got dressed up and made sure he knew what he was missing. And now this! He betrays me with that... that tart! She's working to get me out of here before Lonnie's even cold."

"Chelsea wasn't looking for information to get you out of the house," I said. Although, she was interested in grabbing as many of Lonnie's assets as she could, including this mysterious gold Sylvia had told me about.

"I think she cheated on Lonnie when they were together." Elita continued as if she hadn't heard me. "She didn't deserve him, or any of this."

"I'm done with this dress," Helen said. "Do you want to change into the next one? I'll alter that as well."

Elita shrugged out of the dress Helen had altered and held her hand out for the next one, standing in front of me in her fitted black slip.

I admired Elita's confidence. I hated trying on clothes in communal changing rooms, but Elita wasn't fazed by us being there while she stood in her underwear.

"I need this dress ready as soon as possible." Elita smoothed the fabric over her thighs. "I can't wander around looking like a grieving widow. Since I'm not even Lonnie's widow, what's the point of making a pretense of it? Take the hem up three inches on this one. My legs are my best asset."

Helen shot me a wide-eyed look as she pulled out her pin case and dropped to her knees again.

"So?" Elita fixed me with a fierce gaze. "Tell me exactly what Chelsea wanted."

I still wasn't sure how much to reveal. "I think she was interested in what Lonnie left her in the will."

"The will! I knew it! That's all she's ever been after, getting the most out of the situation. Lonnie left her provided for so she won't go begging. She'd never have married him otherwise. Do you know what the age gap was between them?"

"Ten years?" I guessed.

"More like fifteen," Helen muttered through a mouthful of dress pins.

"Try twenty. She could have been his daughter. Frankly, it's embarrassing for both of them." Elita drew in a big gulp of air. "If only Lonnie hadn't been such an old fool, unable to see past her fake boobs and overly-painted face. He'd have seen there was no heart there, and she didn't love him. Not like I did. Even after Lonnie left me, I still hoped he might realize what a fool he'd been and come back. Even after everything he put me through, I'd have been waiting for him."

Lonnie, who'd been content to listen to our conversation, moved closer to Elita, his head lowered.

"Men can be idiots, sometimes," Helen said.

"Idiots and cheaters," Elita said. "I knew about Lonnie's little indiscretions, but none of them were serious. That was until Chelsea got her claws into him. I knew something was different after they met at a charity cricket match we attended. She wouldn't leave him alone. She even flirted with him while I stood by his side. I should have ripped out her hair extensions and stuck a pin in that too big chest of hers."

"It might have stopped things going any further," I said.

"Looking back, I wish I had," Elita said. "But I figured she was just another of Lonnie's floozies. And besides, he was getting old. He was still handsome, but no longer turned heads the way he used to when he was twenty. He was such a good-looking guy, in his best suit, his hair slicked back, and a gleam of naughtiness in his eyes. Lonnie knocked me right off my feet the first time we met."

"The hem's done." Helen stood and put her pins away.

Lonnie dropped to his knees and ran a hand up Elita's exposed flesh.

"Oh! Yes, my dress. Thank you, Helen." Elita rested her hands on the desk. "Actually, I feel a bit faint."

I waved Lonnie away, knowing his contact was making Elita feel bad.

He took a long look at Elita's legs before floating away.

Helen grabbed a chair and placed it behind Elita. "Take a seat. You do look pale." She looked at me and mouthed the word *ghost*?

I nodded, keeping a close eye on Lonnie to make sure he didn't return for another feel of his ex-wife's legs.

Elita sank into the chair and rested her head in her hands. "I'm finding this so stressful. I didn't think I'd care when Lonnie died. Why should I after everything he did to me? It's such a shock the way it happened."

"It sounds like a horrible accident," I said.

A sob shot out of Elita, and she clamped a hand over her mouth. "It's my fault."

I raised my eyebrows and looked at Helen. "You had something to do with Lonnie's death?"

"I loved him, but I must have wished him dead a dozen times," Elita said. "And now, I feel terrible. I forced my wishes into reality. I killed Lonnie."

I walked around the desk and patted Elita's shoulder. "You wishing something will happen doesn't mean it will. I sometimes wish Helen wouldn't sing so loudly in the shower, but it won't change her noisy off-key singing every morning."

"Lorna, that's not appropriate." Helen glared at me. "I have a lovely singing voice."

"It's more than that." Elita wiped tears from her cheeks. "My family descended from Romany gypsies. We were a strong and powerful family. And we have... abilities."

"What kind of abilities?" Helen asked.

"I had an aunt who could predict the future," Elita said. "She knew I would marry Lonnie."

"Maybe your aunt knew that because she saw the two of you together and decided you were a good match," I said.

"No. That wasn't a one-off. She was always doing it. It was a spooky ability of hers. My mother was the same. She could see things before they happened. And if anybody fell out with her, something bad always happened to them. You never went to sleep on an argument you had with my mom. If you did, the next day you'd wake with a face covered in pimples."

"You make it sound as if you hexed Lonnie," Helen said. "Do you have these abilities too?"

"I didn't think so, but I must have." Elita nodded, her eyes red-rimmed as more tears fell. "That's what I did. I wished him dead. You can't take a hex back once you've cast it."

"For a hex to work, you'd have to mean it," I said. "I have bad thoughts sometimes, but that doesn't mean I want the horrid things that pop into my head to happen. I don't blame you for feeling bitter toward Lonnie, though. It sounds as if he didn't treat you well."

Elita nodded. "He was always one extreme or the other. Lonnie could have a heart of gold or a heart of ice. His moods changed so quickly, and I never knew what to expect. I suppose that was a part of his charm. He kept me on my toes. I was never bored when I was with him. I wish he'd felt the same when it came to me."

"I'm sure he loved you." I looked at Lonnie, and he nodded several times.

"He did," Elita said, "especially when we were first together. He was like my swan. You know, they mate for life?"

"I didn't know that," I said. We'd moved from family hexes to bird mating behavior at a head spinning rate.

"I wasn't his swan, though." Elita grabbed a hanky from the box on the desk and dabbed her eyes and nose. "I wish I'd been good enough for him."

"You were more than good enough for him," Helen said. "You stood by him when he was silly enough to get himself thrown into prison. You never complained when he cheated, and even when he divorced you and married Chelsea, you stayed and made sure his final farewell was a good one."

"You must think I'm a fool." Elita blinked up at Helen.

"I think you were a woman in love," Helen said. "And love makes people do ridiculous things. You stood by your man, stood by the person you thought was your soulmate. I have to admire you for that."

"Lonnie's the fool in all of this. He didn't know what an amazing woman he had until he'd lost you." I looked over to where Lonnie stood. His head was bowed, and his hands clasped in front of him as if he was in mourning. And perhaps he was. Having heard Elita talk about her lost love and how much she missed him, he would have to be a heartless individual not to feel anything.

"I hope Lonnie realizes his mistakes," Helen said.

I gestured discreetly to the corner Lonnie was in and nodded at Helen. "If he were able to, I'm sure he'd want to make amends. That must be why he gave you half the house."

"I'd give up all of my jewels, my expensive clothes, and even this house to have Lonnie back," Elita said. "For all his faults, I'd still forgive him."

Lonnie raised his head and pressed one hand over his heart.

"I don't think you have anything to worry about in regards to your hex killing Lonnie," I said. "It sounds as if he had a few enemies."

"You're right about that." Elita gave me a quizzical look as she dried the last of her tears. "Why should that matter? If I didn't hex him, it was just a tragic accident."

"Oh, of course it was," I said. "I didn't mean anything by that. Simply that other people might have wished him dead as well. I'm sure you weren't the only one to say angry words about Lonnie."

Elita snuffled into the hanky. "I guess so. You know, your references didn't mention how well you deal with emotionally messed up middle-aged women. I've plunged you headlong into a family drama. Neither of you blinked. You're both still here. For that, I'm grateful."

I guessed word hadn't gotten back to Elita that we'd tried to vanish in the middle of the night. "We're happy to help."

"You're both good girls," Elita said. "And you deserve a reward."

I hoped she wasn't going to pull out a wedge of cash and give it to me. It seemed to be something of a trend in this household.

"We're going to have a fun evening." Elita straightened her spine and smiled. "I have a good feeling about you both. I like you already. We must solidify our friendship with cocktails and fun. It's time for you girls to get your glad rags on."

Chapter 9

I blinked in surprise at Elita. "We don't need a party. We're only doing our jobs."

Helen frowned at me. "But a few cocktails would be nice."

"Absolutely," Elita said as she patted Helen's arm. "You've already done such a great job on the dresses I've given you. I need to show one off this evening. And you two will be there by my side when I do so. I'll get us some fancy food, as well. What's your favorite?"

"Thai," Helen said.

"Mexican," I said.

"Well, my favorite is Italian," Elita said. "I'm assuming you both like pizza?"

"Sure. Who doesn't love pizza?" I said.

"Then it's a date." Elita stood. "I'm feeling better already. I have something to look forward to."

"Where's the party taking place?" Helen bounced on her toes. Nothing made her happier than exotic cocktails and plenty of food.

"Meet me in the dining room in two hours," Elita said. "And make sure you both dress up. We're going to have a fun evening getting to know each other. I'll invite the rest of the family, too. You didn't get the chance to meet everybody yesterday. This will be your opportunity."

A little of the pleasure I felt faded at the thought of having to spend the evening with the scheming Chelsea and the intimidating Carson. I couldn't think of a decent enough excuse to get out of the party before Elita left the room, and let out a sigh as I looked at Helen.

"What?" she asked. "You're not going to turn down cocktails, are you?"

"I wouldn't have minded the cocktails if it was just the three of us," I said.

Helen wrinkled her nose. "Yes, it might not be such a great night now. But it will give us a chance to get to know people and do some digging about Lonnie and everyone's motives for wanting him dead."

"I'm going to take a stab in the dark and say the missing gold has something to do with it." I looked over to see Lonnie still lurking in the corner of the room. "Lonnie's been with me all day and has made it clear he didn't think much of Chelsea. She'd be a good place to start."

"Elita also hates her," Helen said. "Can you believe she stuck by her man after everything he did?"

"Like you said, she loved him. She must still care for him to put up with everything going on here."

"Come on," Helen said. "We'd better get ourselves ready for an evening of sleuthing and sea breeze cocktails."

I trudged up the stairs with Helen, Flipper trailing along behind me. Even he didn't seem excited by the thought of free food at tonight's party.

We'd only been in my room for a couple of minutes figuring out what to wear, when there was a knock on the door, and Elita opened it.

"I thought you girls might like something to brighten up your outfits." She handed over two small pink boxes.

I took mine and pulled off the lid, letting out a gasp as I saw what was inside. A diamond necklace stared back at me. This had obscenely expensive sparkling all over it.

Elita laughed and gestured at Helen. "Your turn now."

Helen opened her box and pulled out a diamond choker. "Wow! These are stunning."

"I've got more diamonds than I know what to do with," Elita said. "And these will look beautiful on you. Consider them a loan while you're here. Just make sure you take care of them. That's a lot of money to hang around your pretty necks. Whatever you do, don't let Chelsea anywhere near them. She drools every time she sees me in my diamonds." Elita flashed us a huge diamond on her ring finger.

"I'm not sure I can wear this." I brushed my fingers over the cold diamonds. "I don't want to risk damaging it."

"Impossible. You can't break a diamond," Elita said. "You must wear the necklace. It's my treat to you, another way of saying thank you for helping me when I made such a mess of myself. I don't usually fall apart so easily. I let myself down."

"You didn't." I took out the necklace and held it up. The diamonds sparkled in the bedroom light. "And these are lovely."

"Well, I must go sort out my own outfit. I'll see you girls downstairs soon." Elita turned and hurried out of the bedroom, shutting the door behind her as she did so.

"Blimey! Imagine the kind of gifts we'll get if we do an outstanding job," Helen said as she tried on the choker and looked at her reflection in the mirror on the dresser.

"The family is keen on giving you things for doing work for them," I said. "It's like they've forgotten we get a wage for being here. And I meant to tell you, when Chelsea was in the study with me earlier, she gave me money to keep her informed about what I was doing with Elita and Lonnie's paperwork."

"She wants you to spy on the family?" Helen asked. "You didn't agree, did you?"

"I didn't get a chance to say no," I said. "She pulled out this enormous bundle of money, thrust it at me, and left. I'm not sure what she's expecting me to find, but she mentioned gold."

"Gold! Is she after the family treasure? The gold Lonnie allegedly pinched?"

"She must be, although she was deliberately vague about it."

"Everyone wants Lonnie's gold. I can't say I blame them. A couple of gold bar would come in handy with all the money we're spending on our new home." Helen pulled open my closet and rifled through my clothes. "You should wear your little black dress tonight. It'll go perfectly with your new jewels."

"I'm afraid to wear my necklace in case I damage it. It must be insured for hundreds of thousands of pounds."

"Just make sure you don't get into any fights," Helen said. "Then you won't risk getting it damaged. You have to wear the necklace or you'll offend Elita."

"I will wear it. I do like Elita, but we need to consider her a suspect in Lonnie's murder."

Helen handed me my black dress. "Both the wife and the ex-wife would gain a lot from Lonnie being dead. And they'd both have had easy access to his bathroom. Either of them could have snuck in and thrown the radio in the bath water. They knew his routine, so they'd just have to time it right so no one was around when they committed the evil deed."

"You don't think they worked together to get rid of Lonnie?" I shimmied out of my work clothes and into my black dress. "Maybe the two of them hating each other is an act. They realized that with Lonnie gone, they could have all his assets. They might have a plan to divide everything between them."

"I'm not so sure," Helen said. "Their hatred for each other has to be genuine."

I nodded as I zipped myself into my dress and smoothed down the front. "They do despise each other. I don't think any amount of money would make you that good of an actress."

Helen shut my closet door. "Tonight will help us decide who's most likely to have killed Lonnie."

"Make sure you keep your questioning discreet," I said. "This family is not to be messed with. And if Gunner discovers anything dubious about them, we're out of here, no matter how much Lonnie begs us to stay."

"I bet all he finds are a few parking fines."

"Didn't you hear Elita talking about Lonnie going inside?" I said. "You don't get six months for a few parking fines."

"I bet it was something to do with tax evasion," Helen said.

"They got the Godfather for tax evasion," I said, "and he was a big-time criminal."

"The Cornells are nothing like the Corleones," Helen said. "Stop putting scary ideas in my head. I need to get ready. I'm looking forward to cocktail hour."

Helen left me on my own, and I freshened my makeup before finding a pair of suitable black shoes to go with my dress and diamonds.

An hour later, I was standing outside the dining room door with Helen and Flipper. Helen looked fabulous in a scarlet dress, her blonde curls floating around her face and her red lips perfectly painted.

Even Flipper looked smart. I'd brushed his fur and tied a jaunty red and white spotted neckerchief around his throat.

"Are you ready?" I asked, feeling a flutter of nerves in my stomach.

"Let's go catch ourselves a killer." Helen pushed open the door.

The dining room was already set up for the party, and servers were bustling around with trays of food, placing them on the table, along with drinks, plates, and cutlery. It looked like Elita had been serious about getting Italian food. There were several covered silver dishes, and I could smell the rich tang of basil and tomato in the air.

As we walked into the room, I almost ran into a waiter with a plate piled high with calzones.

"Over here, girls." Elita was on the other side of the room with a large pink cocktail in one hand. "You look fabulous. And the diamonds are perfect." She air kissed us both.

"Thanks for these." My fingers touched the jewels around my neck.

"Now, you both need a huge cocktail. And you must start with a Mojito Special." Elita gestured to Michael, who stepped forward from his rigid position by the wall next to her.

"Michael, get these girls two strong Mojito Specials. Plenty of ice and make sure they have an umbrella." She grinned at us. "I love my drinks to have all the trimmings. It makes them extra fun."

Michael nodded and turned away without a word.

"You've got him well-trained," Helen said.

"Michael's a sweetie," Elita said. "He's like a silent, solid rock. You can rely on him for anything."

"Did he used to work for Lonnie?" I asked, watching as the serving staff gave Michael a wide berth while he walked across the room.

"He did," Elita said. "You could call him Lonnie's muscle. Lonnie was never much for getting his hands dirty, unless he had a personal point to prove. He needed an enforcer, someone who would strike fear in anyone's heart if they decided to make the mistake of crossing the family. That enforcer was Michael. I don't use him for that, now. He's my personal bodyguard. I feel safe when he's nearby."

I looked around the room, thinking I was on the set of some mobster movie. I spotted Chelsea and Ignatius enter the dining room, closely followed by two sunglass wearing bouncer types, one of whom was Hog.

Elita laughed. "I didn't mean to shock you into silence. We aren't all bad. Not anymore, anyway. Lonnie just liked doing things the old-fashioned way. Even though he mellowed as he got older, he stuck to a certain code of conduct."

Michael returned with two pink drinks, complete with umbrella and pineapple garnishes, and handed them to Helen and me.

"Get yourself one, as well," Elita said to Michael.

"I'm more of a whiskey man." Michael gave a small smile.

"You must enjoy yourself tonight," Elita said. "We've all been under stress. Now Lonnie has gone, things have to change. No more drama in the family."

"Whatever you say." Michael backed away before turning and moving to the opposite side of the room, his hands in fists as he did so.

Elita sighed as she watched him. "There goes a man who needs to relax. I can't remember the last time Lonnie gave him time off. Stress is a killer. If the bullets don't get you, the stress will."

I opened my mouth but had nothing to add to that strange comment.

Elita smiled at me. "Anyway, what about you girls? Are you looking for men or are you both taken?"

"Lorna's disgustingly in love with a gardener," Helen said.

"That's lovely. It's nice to have a man who knows what to do with his hands." Elita winked at me. "What about you, Helen? Don't tell me no one has snapped you up."

"Helen's disgustingly single." I grinned wickedly at her. "But she is looking for love."

"Oh! I have just the solution for that. An eligible bachelor you might like. He's mature and wealthy," Elita said.

"Helen likes older guys," I said.

Elita looked around the room, and her eyes brightened. "Ignatius, come here and chat to Helen."

Helen's jaw dropped, and she snapped it shut as a squat, heavyset man with cropped hair and stubble looked over. He had gold chains on his wrist and around his neck.

"That's okay. You don't need to do any matchmaking for me," Helen said.

"Nonsense. I'm happy to help," Elita said. She beckoned Ignatius over. He approached slowly, his dark eyes narrowed. "And don't worry about him. He seems a little rough around the edges, but he has his priorities right and puts the family first. And he's loyal. You can't do better than that."

Helen shot me a pleading look, but I could do nothing but smile and sip my drink. This should be interesting. Helen did like older guys, but this was Lonnie's brother, and he gave off the same air of menace as the rest of the family.

Elita caught hold of Ignatius's elbow and moved him so he stood next to Helen. "Are you enjoying our little gathering?"

Ignatius looked around. "Not many here."

"It's early," Elita said. "My cousins should be here in the next half hour. And it is an impromptu get together, so it'll be small and intimate. I thought it would be fun."

Ignatius shrugged. "My brother always enjoyed a party."

"Don't you think Helen is looking lovely tonight?" Elita asked.

Ignatius glanced at Helen, and his gaze ran over her. "I like your diamonds."

"They're on loan," Helen squeaked.

"They make her blue eyes sparkle," Elita said. "And Helen was just telling me she's single. Can you imagine such a pretty girl being without a man?"

Ignatius took a sip of his whiskey. "Some women can be too independent for their own good. It puts a man off."

"Don't be a tease," Elita said. "Helen is a thoroughly modern woman. We're allowed to have jobs now if we choose to."

"I wouldn't want any woman of mine working," Ignatius said. "You never know where they are when they go out to work."

"I expect your girlfriends have all gotten jobs to get away from your controlling nature," Helen said.

"Oh, no!" Elita said. "Ignatius is just protective. It's a good quality to have. It shows he cares."

"I'd rather my husband trusted me enough to go out to work, without thinking I was getting into mischief," Helen said.

"Cornell women don't work," Ignatius said. "There's no need."

Elita placed a hand on Ignatius's arm. "Those values might seem old-fashioned, but they've worked well for us. Our men have always been the providers."

I took a sip of my drink. More like controlling idiots who weren't smart enough to deserve anyone as sweet as Elita.

"Which is fine until they leave you." Chelsea strolled over, wearing a green tube dress, a cat-like smirk on her face. "You spent your valuable years being a pampered useless bag of silicone-filled fakeness. What is it you spend your time doing now you're a middle-aged ex-wife, Elita?"

Elita scowled. "I'm looking after Lonnie's estate. Nobody else wants to take an interest. I refuse to let it be ruined by those more interested in dividing up his assets than keeping the family honor intact."

"I would be involved if I hadn't been elbowed out the way," Chelsea said. "And have you told me yet when you're moving out? I fancy a good bonfire, and can use your raggedy clothes as fuel."

"I'll stay as long as I choose to," Elita said. "You know that's what Lonnie wanted."

Chelsea shook her head. "This is a marital home, not a place for worn out old nags."

Everyone inhaled at the same time, just waiting for the fight to begin.

"Why are you even here?" Elita asked, her tone even. "I don't remember issuing you an invitation to come to drinks."

"Ignatius told me you were having a little gathering. I assumed my invitation had been lost." Chelsea's gaze shifted to me. "How are you enjoying working for Elita?"

"Very much," I said as I remembered the money Chelsea had tried to bribe me with.

"Lorna and Helen are fitting in well," Elita said. "Don't try poisoning their minds against me."

Chelsea gave me an exaggerated wink. "It's important I get to know my new members of staff."

"You're paying their wages, are you?" Elita spat.

"Lonnie's money is paying them. Therefore, I must be," Chelsea said. "After all, I am his actual wife."

Ignatius cleared his throat. "Ladies, isn't this supposed to be an evening where we enjoy ourselves?"

"It should be," Elita said. "But Miss Botoxed Forehead always likes to spoil things."

"It's Mrs. Botoxed Forehead to you." Chelsea flashed her wedding ring at Elita.

I hid my smile behind my giant pink drink. So far, everyone was acting in their usual crazy way. This evening could be either interesting or horribly stressful.

"Chelsea, go see where Carson has got to," Ignatius said. "He said he'd be joining us."

"He's big enough and ugly enough to look after himself," Chelsea said.

"Be a good girl. Just go and check for me," he said.

Chelsea glared at Ignatius. "Go find him yourself." She turned on her overly high heels and strutted away.

"Thank you, Ignatius," Elita said. "Chelsea must have been raised by wolves. She has no concept of good manners or decorum." She sucked the cherry off the end of her drink's umbrella.

"Chelsea has her good points." Ignatius's eyes were glued to Chelsea's backside as it wobbled under the tight fabric of her dress.

"Typical man," Helen muttered.

"I enjoy a good-looking woman." Ignatius tore his gaze from Chelsea's curves.

"Well, you can keep your eyes off my curves," Helen said. "I'm spoken for."

"I thought you were looking for love," Elita said.

"I have someone interested in me," Helen said. "I'm deciding if he's the right one for me. I've wasted too many dates and too many kisses on losers. The next man I date I intend to marry."

I looked at Helen in surprise. Was she referring to Gunner? Every time I tried to get her to open up about him, she insisted he was nothing more than an annoyance. Did she really have marriage in mind when she looked at him? No wonder she was struggling to make up her mind.

"Tell me everything about this man." Elita's eyes sparkled. "I do enjoy a good love story. Why do you think he's not the one for you?"

"He's a bit of a tease," Helen said, shooting me a narrowed eyed look as if daring me to say anything. "And he always jokes around. He can't be serious for more than a few minutes."

"Some men are like that," Elita said. "It takes a good woman by their side to make them grow up and give them something to fight for."

"And his work takes him away," Helen said. "He's a busy man. He might not have enough time for me. I don't want to end up home on my own all the time, wondering if he's okay."

"What does he do?" Elita asked. "He's not in the army, is he? They send our boys away for months on end. It must drive their wives mad not knowing where they are or even if they're safe."

"Nothing like that," Helen said. "He's in the police."

The conversation in the room died. All eyes swiveled to stare at Helen.

The piece of pizza Ignatius was holding fell to the floor with a plop.

Helen licked her lips and stared around the room. "What just happened?"

"We're not fans of law enforcement," Ignatius said darkly. "If I'd have known a cop was sniffing around you, I wouldn't have wasted my time even speaking to you."

Helen blinked several times and gave me a puzzled look. "I'm not dating him yet."

"It's better if you don't date him at all." Elita gave Helen's hand a brief pat, a worried look in her eyes. "We've had a few run-ins with the law over the years. It always ends badly, often for them."

"There's always some cop wanting to put me away," Ignatius said. "It's a disgrace the way they've hounded this family over the years."

"Why would they hound you?" I asked.

"Because they've got it in for us," Ignatius said. "Police hold grudges and never let you forget if you've done something wrong."

"Our wrong doings are in the past," Elita said. "All we want is a quiet life."

"Having a member of staff dating a cop is out of the question," Ignatius said.

Helen cleared her throat pointedly. "You can't dictate who I date."

"Well, that's true, but think carefully before you date him," Elita said. "Life as the girlfriend of a police officer must be stressful."

It couldn't be any more stressful than being married to a criminal. I sipped more of my sweet cocktail and decided not to air that thought.

"That's part of the reason I'm ignoring him," Helen said.

"My advice is to keep ignoring him and look elsewhere," Elita said. "You don't want that pretty face lined with worry wrinkles."

Helen rubbed a finger across her crease-free forehead. "I guess not."

Flipper ran over from his investigation of the food table, sat at Ignatius's feet, and pointed his nose at the piece of dropped pizza.

Ignatius looked down and ruffled Flipper's fur. "It's all yours, boy. Hope you like pepperoni."

Flipper made short work of the pizza before looking up again and raising a paw at Ignatius. Flipper definitely did like pepperoni.

Ignatius laughed, and the tension in the room faded as people continued their conversations.

"I've always liked dogs," Ignatius said. "This one is smart. He sees an opportunity and goes for it."

"He's the smartest dog I've ever met." My shoulders inched down as Ignatius switched on the charm and began complimenting Elita on her dress.

Here was a man to watch out for. There was something dark lurking behind his gaze, and I could see through his charming words and didn't like what hid behind them. I was adding him to my suspect list.

Sylvia shot through the doorway in her wheelchair, Reggie sitting on her lap and yapping loudly. The wheels of her chair skidded across the polished floor. "He's here! My boy is here!"

We all looked at her in surprise.

"Who are you talking about, Sylvia?" Elita asked.

"It's Lonnie!" Sylvia's silver-gray hair was a fluffy mess around her head. "He's outside. He's after the gold!"

Chapter 10

"The gold!" Ignatius set down his drink and hurried outside.

Sylvia was already manoeuvring her wheelchair around, seeming determined to get out the front door as quickly as possible.

"Wait a second." Elita grabbed the back of Sylvia's chair to prevent her from leaving. "Did you say it was Lonnie outside?"

"That's right. I saw him with my own eyes," Sylvia said.

"She's almost blind," Carson muttered.

"He was right in front of me!" Sylvia glared at Carson. "And my hearing is excellent, so watch what you say. Lonnie is out there. He was gesturing for me to follow him. He's come back to tidy up the loose ends. That includes making sure everyone knows how he really died."

Elita knelt next to the wheelchair and took hold of Sylvia's hand. "Lonnie's dead. We just laid him to rest."

"I'm telling you, he was outside." Sylvia's wild gaze shot to me. "She'll back me up. Lorna knows what I'm talking about."

I took a step back. There was no way I was revealing my ghost seeing ability in front of the family.

"Let's take a look outside and see what's going on. It could be we have an intruder in the grounds who scared you." Michael strode to the door.

"I know my own son when I see him," Sylvia said, "even if he is a ghost."

"You ladies stay here. I'll go investigate." Michael headed toward the front door.

"There's no way I'm staying in here," I muttered to Helen. "Let's go see what Sylvia's talking about."

We abandoned our drinks and hurried to the front door, which stood open, an unwelcoming inky blackness looming outside.

I took a deep breath, ignoring the nerves fluttering in my chest, and walked outside with Helen and Flipper.

Michael stood in front of the water fountain outside, slowly scanning the grounds. His hands were balled into fists as if he was preparing to strike an enemy the second he spotted one.

Ignatius stood to the right of Michael, his hands stuffed into his pants pockets as he looked around.

"Do you see Lonnie?" Helen whispered, her fingers gripping my arm.

I looked around the garden. There was that unsettling same sensation again, like I was staring at trouble and it had me in its sights. "If he was here, I don't think he is anymore. Maybe Sylvia scared him off."

"What about the gold?" Helen asked. "Do you think Lonnie has come back to get it?"

"There's not much use for gold where he's going," I said. "But he might have plans about what he wants done with it."

We turned toward the sound of raised female voices. Sylvia rolled her wheelchair into the front garden, and Elita hurried behind her.

"I need to see if he's still out here," Sylvia snapped at Elita. "If my Lonnie needs help, I'm going to give it to him."

"Lonnie's at rest now," Elita said, a worried look on her face. "There's nothing anyone can do for him."

"I don't believe that," Sylvia said. "He wouldn't be around if he was at peace. And we all know the reason he can't rest."

Ignatius stalked over and glared at Sylvia. "You don't know what you're talking about, Mom."

"Of course I do," Sylvia said. "Lonnie didn't hide anything from me. He was a good boy. I always said you could learn a lot from him."

"He was my younger brother," Ignatius said. "He should have been learning from me. If he'd taken some of my advice, he might still be alive."

"You've got enough bullet holes in you to know you're more lucky than clever," Sylvia said. Her gaze moved to Helen and me, and she beckoned us closer. "You girls need to know everything about this family. You won't be able to help Lonnie, otherwise."

"Mom, you shouldn't tell anyone else about family matters," Ignatius said.

"They should be told," Elita said. "The girls need to know who they're working for."

I took a deep breath. "What's the truth?"

No one spoke for several seconds.

"Lonnie masterminded a gold heist," Elita said on a sigh.

I pulled my face into what I hoped looked like I was shocked, and not that Sylvia had already dropped that golden bombshell on Helen and me almost as soon as we'd arrived.

"Well, that's what everyone believes," Sylvia said slyly. She gave me a knowing nod.

"He had some help," Ignatius muttered.

"You hush now," Sylvia snapped. "You know Lonnie wanted to do this one big job before he retired. He knew it would set us up for life. It was why he did it. Like I said, he was such a good boy."

"He wasn't that good," Ignatius said. "He hid the gold from us."

"I had a bad feeling that gold would bring us trouble," Elita said.

"Let me tell the story." Sylvia shifted in her wheelchair and placed her hands on her lap, Reggie hopping into the circle her hands made. "You girls can decide what you want to do with the information."

I looked over at Helen, and she nodded. It seemed she was happy to play along as well.

"This family has always trodden along some shady lines when it came to money," Sylvia said. "But we were always honest about what we did."

"Not to the police," Ignatius mumbled.

Sylvia glared at him, and he dropped his head down. "As Lonnie matured, his interest in crime faded. He could see that having too much money wasn't a good thing, but he wanted to make sure we were provided for before he hung up his criminal hat."

"So, we set up a gold heist," Ignatius said. "It took us two years to plan."

"I'm getting to that bit," Sylvia said. "Both my boys worked hard. We had people go undercover so we could work out the routines and weaknesses when the gold was transferred. It was a huge risk, but we knew the reward would be worth it."

"And it was," Ignatius said. "We made off with over twenty-five million pounds worth of gold bars."

"If you believe the rumors." Sylvia arched an eyebrow as she stared at me and Helen. "Because the gold has never been found."

I swallowed, realizing I'd just heard a confession about a robbery.

"Then the problems began," Sylvia said. "Keeping a lot of stolen gold bars was risky, so Lonnie was tasked with making sure the gold disappeared."

"And that's exactly what he did," Ignatius said. "We transferred the gold into three vehicles, then they vanished into the night. That was the last I ever saw any of the gold."

"We might not have seen any of the actual gold bars," Sylvia said, "but Lonnie was generous with his money. He was drip feeding it to the family so as not to alert the police."

"That sounds sensible," I said, realizing how dry my throat felt.

"He was a clever boy," Sylvia said. "He was doing what was best for us all."

"He had us under his control." Ignatius slapped a hand on his thigh. "He wouldn't tell anyone where the gold was."

"The fact we don't know where this gold is, is a good thing," Sylvia said. "If there's no proof, then no one can take the blame."

"That's also sensible," I said.

"Of course, the police were hot on our tail for ages trying to find out information," Sylvia said. "They had nothing to go on. My boys are so smart, they left nothing behind, no clues, and no evidence that they were involved."

"The police have closed the investigation?" Helen asked.

"And it will stay closed," Ignatius said. "If I discover it's been re-opened, I'll be coming to you first and asking who you've been blabbing to. If you go sweet talking to your cop boyfriend about this that will be the end for you."

"As if I would." Helen glared at Ignatius.

"Now, you don't go threatening either of the girls," Sylvia said. "I trust them. And besides, we've just told them a story. It's not as if we've handed them a gold bar to go running to the police with."

"We won't tell anybody," I said, noticing the dark look in Ignatius's eyes. "As Sylvia was quick to point out, there's no proof any of you were involved. We'd gain nothing by going to the police and telling them this information."

"Especially not when it comes from a crazy old lady," Ignatius muttered.

"You're not too old for me to bend over my knee and give you a good spanking," Sylvia said.

"I'd like to see you try." Ignatius turned and walked away.

"That boy! I thought I'd raised him better," Sylvia said, before looking at me and Helen. "The tale doesn't end there."

"What else is there to tell?" Elita asked.

"Something must be wrong. Lonnie is still here," Sylvia said.

Elita sighed. "That's not possible."

"He's here for two reasons," Sylvia continued. "Because he wants his gold to come to the family, and he wants his killer brought to justice."

Elita frowned. "Lonnie's death was an accident, and the gold has gone. He probably melted it down and sold it off and there's a stack of money invested somewhere we'll never find."

"We'll find it," Sylvia said. "Lonnie won't let us down."

"Sylvia, there's no such thing as ghosts," Elita said. "You must have seen somebody wandering around and made a mistake."

"I know what I saw," Sylvia said. "Lorna, you can see him as well."

"I can't see Lonnie out here," I said reluctantly.

Sylvia tutted and shook her head.

"Of course you can't," Elita said, sharpness in her voice. "Lonnie's ashes are sitting in an urn in my bedroom."

"Shouldn't Chelsea have the urn?" Ignatius asked from his safe spot far away from his mother.

"She said the ashes repulsed her." Elita snorted and shook her head. "Some wife she turned out to be. She'll never be a true Cornell."

"My Lonnie would agree with you," Sylvia said. "The next time I see him, I'm going to ask what he wants done with his ashes."

"No, you don't," Elita snapped, "because he's not here. He's dead. You claiming you can see him is only making everything worse."

"You know I don't lie," Sylvia said.

The two women glared at each other before Sylvia sighed and raised her gaze to meet mine. "Let's not fight over this. It's not what Lonnie would have wanted."

"I suppose you're going to check that with him, as well." Elita took a step toward Michael. "Was there anyone out here when you came to take a look?"

"No one," Michael said. "The place is secure. I'll check around Lonnie's military vehicles and make sure no one has been tampering with them."

"See!" Elita turned to Sylvia. "We're alone. No one is trying to get to the gold. Dead or alive."

Sylvia waved away Elita's comment and faced me. "Now you know our history, do you still want to stay here?"

"Do stay. We might have a crooked edge," Elita said, "but we have a heart of gold."

Sylvia grinned. "We will when we find it."

"We're a hard-working family, who take what's owed to us," Ignatius said as he re-joined the group. "There's nothing wrong with that."

I couldn't agree with him on that point. Nobody needed that much gold. That was just being greedy.

"Stay a week and see how you get on," Elita said. "I like you girls. I think you'll do well here."

"So long as you both keep your mouths shut about Mom's gold heist story," Ignatius sneered. "Remember, you can't get anything to stick if you tell that tale to anyone else."

"Boy, I'm warning you," Sylvia said. "Stop threatening the girls, or we're going to fall out. I can cut your allowance, you know."

I stifled a smile as Ignatius slumped forward. My gaze settled on Sylvia, who peered at me with interest.

"If we find the gold, maybe we can cut you in on the deal," Sylvia said, "make you permanent staff."

"No way!" Ignatius said. "They had nothing to do with it."

"Oh! No thanks. I wouldn't have the first clue what to do with a bar of gold," I said.

"We wouldn't give you one of those. If we did, you wouldn't need to work anymore," Elita said, "unless you like being here."

"I like working," I said.

"Stubborn, modern women," Ignatius growled.

Helen squeaked with indignation, but I grabbed her arm to stop her starting another argument with Ignatius. "I think we've had enough fun for one night."

"It has been revealing," Sylvia said, a twinkle in her dark eyes.

"You'll be here in the morning?" Elita asked. "I've so appreciated your help today. I do need you both, even if it's just until things settle and I get used to not having Lonnie around."

I was torn between the desire to get as far away from these criminals as I could and the urge to help Elita. Here was a woman grieving the loss of her cheating ex-husband. She needed someone stable by her side, someone who wasn't going around looking menacing all the time or shouting about ghosts and disrupting the family with tales of gold heists. There was also the matter of Lonnie's murder to solve.

"We'll stay." I looked at Helen. "Won't we?"

"I'm happy if you are," she said.

"That's excellent news." Elita gave me a relieved smile. "Now, let me tempt you both to one more cocktail."

"Yes. Maybe something with strong spirits to keep the ghosts away." Sylvia glared at me.

"We've had enough for one night," I said, refusing to feel bad for not admitting I could see Lonnie's ghost.

We said a hasty good night and left the family to continue drinking.

"We're sharing a bed again, aren't we?" Helen asked, as we reached my bedroom door.

"Absolutely," I said. "There's no way I'm going to risk sleeping alone in this house."

"That's what I was thinking," Helen said. "What with Lonnie's ghost on the prowl, and Ignatius issuing covert threats at every opportunity, I don't think I'm ever going to want to sleep alone again."

Chapter 11

The next morning, I woke feeling groggy. The cocktail I'd had last night had been strong. Coupled with that, Helen had hogged the covers most of the night. At one point, I'd ended up squashed on the edge of the mattress, hugging Flipper to keep me warm. I wasn't sure how much longer we'd be sharing a bed if she kept this up.

"So, last night was interesting." Helen shut my bedroom door behind her, having come from her room after getting showered and dressed.

"There were plenty of suspects in Lonnie's death," I said.

"The ex-wife and the wife," Helen said.

"And the older brother," I said. "He'd benefit if they can find this gold. And Michael. And Carson. We've got so many suspects to investigate."

"Sylvia is clever," Helen said. "She didn't let on that she'd already told us about the gold. And everything we heard last night could have been made up."

"With no evidence of actual gold, we've got nothing useful to go on."

"With Lonnie dead, the family must be desperate to know where he hid it."

"It can't be easy to hide so many gold bars. You wouldn't be able to hide them in a bag in the back of the closet."

"Maybe Lonnie's got a secret room in the house where the gold is stashed," Helen said.

"If the police were that interested in them for the heist, they'd have searched every inch of this place," I said, "including pulling up drawings of house designs and making sure there were no places the gold could be tucked away. I bet Gunner can tell us where they searched."

Helen groaned and sank onto my bed. "Don't go getting him involved in this."

"He's already involved," I said. "You know I asked him to look into the Cornells."

"Has he found out anything useful?" Helen asked.

"Let's find out." I rang Gunner's number, but it went straight to voicemail. I hung up and tried Zach. He answered after the second ring.

"I was about to call you," he said. "I wanted to make sure nothing bad happened to you, given you're working for a criminal mastermind."

"They're not masterminds," I said. "And as much as I love talking to you, I'm after Gunner. I wanted to see if he had an update about the Cornells."

"He's with me at the house. I know he's been looking into them. From what I've heard, it's not good news."

I sucked in a breath. "What did he find out?"

"The family is scarily hardcore. You need to get out of there before something bad happens to you."

"Define scarily hardcore?" I looked at Helen and saw the worried expression on her face. It mirrored my own concerns. "They've mentioned a few things from their past. You're not going to tell me they're some kind of serial killer family."

"Nothing like that," Zach said. "But they all have records, even the old lady."

"What for?"

"Give me the phone." I could hear Gunner's voice in the background.

"Hold on a second," Zach said.

"Hey, Lorna," Gunner said. "Listen, this family has been on our radar for years. The Cornells have got their fingers in lots of unsavory pies."

"Like what?"

"Money-laundering, robbery, GBH. They used to run a car racketeering business in the seventies but moved into robbing security vans instead. That's where they made their big money. They're not a family to be messed with."

"I'm figuring that out," I said.

"Have they caused you any trouble?" Gunner's tone was sharp.

"They've been good to us," I said. "But it's an odd setup."

"I imagine it is," Gunner said. "Be careful. You don't want to get on the wrong side of any of them."

"We're doing our best not to," I said.

"What about Helen?" Gunner asked. "I know what a firecracker she can be when someone annoys her. Make sure she keeps her mouth shut."

"Helen isn't going to pay any attention to what you tell her," I said.

"What's he saying about me?" Helen hissed.

"He's telling you to be your usual charming self," I said.

Helen made an unimpressed grumbling sound and folded her arms over her chest. Gunner always knew how to press her buttons.

"I'm not joking around here," Gunner said. "If you think you're in trouble, get out of there."

"Will do," I said. I decided not to mention we still had no idea where Helen's car was, and if we had to escape, it would be on foot.

"If you are staying, I need your help," Gunner said.

"With what?" I asked.

"Now you're on the inside with the Cornells, you can find out information we can use to get them for the crimes they've committed."

My heart sped up. "I'm not sure we can do that. You just told us how dangerous the family is and we need to be careful. Isn't poking around, asking questions about their criminal backgrounds, the opposite of that?"

"Hold on," Gunner said.

I could hear Zach's low murmuring in the background and could imagine what he thought of the idea of us snooping on the Cornells.

"It's safe," Gunner said. "All you need to do is have a discreet dig around and report back anything you find to me. Don't go looking for anything incriminating, but if you stumble across it, make a copy and give it to me."

I still hated the idea. "What sort of thing do you want us to look for?"

"Anything to do with the robberies," Gunner said. "They're wanted for a twenty-five-million-pound gold heist. That's what we're really interested in."

"Wow! A gold heist." I felt bad playing dumb with Gunner, but without any proof, there was no point getting him excited.

"We know they were involved, but they're clever. They had family members working on the inside who conveniently disappeared the day of the gold heist."

I covered the mouthpiece of the phone. "The gold heist story is real," I said to Helen.

"We already knew that," Helen said. "Hasn't Gunner got anything useful for us?"

"What are you saying?" Gunner asked.

"I don't know how much help we'll be in terms of hunting out the gold," I said. "If the police couldn't get anywhere, what's to say we will?"

"You don't need to find the gold, but you're on the inside," Gunner said. "You can look around places and listen in on conversations. We've never had a chance to do that. The family closes down every time they're questioned. In the end, we had to shut the investigation, but no one was happy about doing that. The first sign of fresh evidence and I'm getting it re-opened. You and Helen can help with that."

There was the sound of scuffling on the other end of the phone, followed by a muffled grunt. "Lorna, you don't have to do this. Ignore Gunner. He's not thinking straight." It was Zach.

"I know we don't have to," I said. "But since we're here, we might as well have a look around. I was planning to have a poke around anyway and see what I could find out about Lonnie's death."

"It's not worth the risk," Zach said. "If any of the family discover what you're doing, you'll be in trouble."

"You make it sound like we're in the middle of a gangster movie." I tried to make light of our situation so as not to worry Zach. "If there's a hint of trouble, we'll get out."

"I don't want you putting yourselves at risk," Zach said, "not over something so trivial."

"Twenty-five million pounds worth of missing gold isn't trivial," Gunner said in the background.

"It's not as important as Lorna or Helen," Zach said.

"We're going to stay for now. There's no danger," I said to Zach. "And if we do find anything useful, I'll report back to Gunner. Don't worry about us. We'll keep our heads down and stay out of trouble."

"I've heard you say that before," Zach grumbled. "And I've also discovered you getting up to all sorts of mischief."

"Which is why you love me," I said. "You'd be bored of a girlfriend who did everything by the book."

"Now you're making yourself sound like a criminal," he said.

"I promise you, we don't want any trouble. We'll look around subtly, and any problems, you'll be the first to know and you can swoop in and save us."

"Make sure you do tell me," Zach said. "Hang on. Gunner's got something else he needs to tell you."

I waited as the phone was passed to Gunner.

"Lorna, you and Helen keep a look out for anything about rented spaces, places where the gold could be stashed."

"Got it."

"And report back on any conversations the family has about meetings away from the house."

"Why is that important?"

"The gang could be meeting to discuss tactics," Gunner said. "It could be an opportunity to round them up and make one of them crack."

"Okay, that makes sense," I said. "Anything else?"

"Well, if you discover any of the actual gold, I need to know."

"I doubt that's going to happen," I said. "And if it does, I might disappear, along with Helen, to some tropical island for the rest of my life."

Gunner chuckled. "And leave Zach behind? Not a chance."

"You never know. I've always been tempted by a life of sand and sun."

Gunner's laughter faded. "Lorna, watch your back. Don't put yourself at risk. If you don't want to do this, I'll understand."

"Don't worry. And I'll keep an eye on Helen, as well, and make sure she doesn't do anything daft."

"As if I would," Helen grumbled.

Gunner laughed again. "She always does daft things. That's why I like her."

I said goodbye to Zach and Gunner and hung up.

"So, what are we doing?" Helen asked. "Is it time to pack our bags and run?"

"No, just the opposite. It looks like we're going undercover."

Chapter 12

After the conversation with Gunner that morning, I was fired up to start hunting for clues to find the gold. But the day had been dull, and I hadn't uncovered any of the family's dark secrets while doing filing and checking the post.

I'd worked in the study all day. Elita had drifted in and out, giving me more tasks to do and signing the letters I'd written. It was a very normal day as a personal assistant. Definitely not the lifestyle of a glamorous undercover agent.

Elita was sprawled on the sofa in one corner of the study, gently snoring, after declaring she needed to do some thinking before dinner. In truth, it sounded as if she was sleeping off the aftereffects of last night's party.

I still had a pile of thank you cards and funeral paperwork to deal with and was writing out some cheques for Elita to sign, when Lonnie popped up next to the sofa.

Flipper ran over, and Lonnie smiled down at him before turning his attention to Elita and prodding her with a finger.

"Leave her alone," I whispered. "She had a hard night."

Lonnie shrugged and continued to prod his sleeping ex-wife, who grunted in response and turned over, flinging one arm over her face as she did so.

"It's your fault she's not doing so well," I said. "Get over here and tell me about the gold you stole."

Lonnie's mouth turned down and he shrugged, before giving Elita one final prod and drifting toward me. He had a look on his face like a spoiled child told he couldn't have his fifth bag of candy.

"Elita still loves you, you know," I said. "You were lucky she didn't drag you through the divorce court and take half of all this. She should have."

Lonnie tilted his head, an expression of mock innocence on his face.

"That won't work on me," I whispered. "You should never have cheated on Elita. She's a good woman. Better than you deserved."

Lonnie looked back at Elita, his gaze shifting up and down her figure. He looked at me and nodded.

"And, you might like to consider where your current wife is," I said to Lonnie. "She's hardly pulling out all the stops to ensure everything runs smoothly around here. In fact, I barely see her unless there's alcohol to be consumed or the possibility of discovering your hidden gold."

Lonnie had the decency to dip his head. Maybe he was finally seeing through Chelsea's extensive backcombing and false lashes.

I stood and shut the study door, before checking Elita was still sleeping. I returned to my seat and faced Lonnie. "I need to know about this gold you pinched. That's the key to your murder. There are a lot of people who'd benefit if they could find where it is."

Lonnie nodded again.

"Was someone trying to get information out of you before you died about where the gold was hidden?"

Lonnie scratched his head and looked around the room.

"It could be they grew tired of you hiding things from them and decided to get you out of the way. It leaves things clear for them to go hunting."

Lonnie's brow wrinkled, and he shook his head.

"No one was questioning you about the gold?"

He held his hands out.

"There's no need to play innocent with me. Your mom told me about the gold heist," I said. "And she tried to drop me in it by telling everyone I could see you. I like Sylvia, but she's got to keep quiet about me being able to see you, or I'll get fired."

Lonnie snapped his fingers together, making the impression of a bird's beak opening and shutting quickly.

"Don't be rude about your mom. You stole that gold."

Lonnie turned his back on me.

"Relax! You can't get into trouble now. You're dead! You may as well admit you did it. And Ignatius as good as said he was involved, butting in with unhelpful comments when your mom was telling me what happened."

He turned around slowly and faced me, a look of resignation in his eyes.

"If we find out who wants the gold the most, you'll have your killer."

Lonnie ran his hands through his dark hair several times before finally nodding.

"Good. So, you stole twenty-five million pounds of gold bars and hid them somewhere no one else would find them?"

He nodded.

Now, I was getting somewhere. "I'm guessing the gold is hidden away from the house. You were doing something to it to turn it into usable funds?"

Lonnie raised his eyebrows.

"I'm more than a pretty face and an amazing typist." I grinned at him. "I don't know much about gold dealing, but I know you can't stroll into a pawnbroker's store with a pile of gold bars and ask to trade them for cash. You have to do something to the gold in order to sell it without people getting suspicious. More specifically, without the police getting suspicious."

Lonnie pressed his lips together. He didn't look happy about me bringing the police into the conversation.

"You need to be honest, or I can't help you." I rested my hands on top of the desk. "Let's start with figuring out who's the most resentful about you keeping the gold from them."

He looked at the ground.

"It has to be someone close to you. Someone who lives here. Given the amount of security in this house, no one would be able to sneak in without an alarm going off. If you had to pick one person from this family most likely to have killed you, who would you choose?"

Lonnie still refused to meet my gaze.

I felt a twinge of sympathy for him. It must be hard to accept that the people you thought loved you might prefer you dead. Twenty-five million pounds would make the most honest person swerve off the right path.

"How about Elita? She's cut up about the fact you treated her so poorly when you were married." I glanced at Elita, who was still snoring on the sofa. "A woman scorned and all that. Maybe you pushed her too far."

Lonnie also looked at Elita and shook his head.

"You did leave her for a younger woman. And you cheated on her more than once. That's going to make anyone angry. She might not have planned to kill you. Perhaps she discovered you in the bath one night and her anger took over."

That comment earned me another shrug. So far, so unhelpful.

"If you don't think it was Elita, what about Chelsea?" I asked. "You don't seem happy in your choice of second wife. And as you saw for yourself yesterday, she's interested in where you hid the gold. She could have married you to get her hands on it, and when you didn't deliver, she got angry and decided to get you out of the way and claim what was hers as your widow."

Lonnie drifted around the room. He seemed more interested in looking at the photographs of himself and his family than trying to find out who had the best motive to murder him.

I took a deep breath. "How about we try someone else? What about your right-hand man, Carson? He has a dark streak. Every time he looks at me, I get the chills. It's like he's plotting some dubious deed in his mind and lets it seep out through his expression."

Lonnie gave me a cheeky grin and gestured at a photograph on the desk. It showed a picture of Lonnie in his early twenties and a young Carson with a thick head of springy dark curls. They had their arms around each other and were smiling at the camera.

"You go back a long way," I said. "Best friends can feel closer than family." I felt like that when it came to Helen. I couldn't imagine her not being around, telling me off for wearing walking boots and cooking me amazing meals.

Lonnie looked at the picture some more.

"When lots of money is involved, people do strange things. It changes a person."

He drifted away from the photo.

"If not Carson, how about Michael?" I asked. "He was your protector and is still looking out for your family."

Lonnie shook his head sharply.

"How long have you known Michael?"

He held up his fingers and flashed them three times.

"Thirty years! He can't be much older than that."

Lonnie mimed a child standing next to him and then patted the imaginary child's head.

"You raised Michael?"

Lonnie snitched his nose and waved his hand in the air.

"He's been with you since he was young. You think he'd remain loyal, no matter how much money could be his?"

Lonnie nodded.

"If you aren't prepared to consider Carson or Michael, then look closer at your family." I glanced at Elita. She was still asleep. "Ignatius mentioned something about you wanting to come clean. That would mean trouble for other people who were involved with your... business dealings. Coming clean about your criminal past would make you unpopular, and others would face the risk of prison."

Lonnie floated to the other side of the desk and pulled open the bottom drawer. He gestured at the contents.

I walked around and took a look. Inside was a large metal box.

He pointed at it and gestured for me to lift it out.

I pulled out the box and opened the lid, discovering a big pile of papers inside. "The Academy for Creative Entrepreneurs." I read through the first page of the document. "This looks like a charity for kids who've gotten into trouble."

Lonnie nodded, a look of pride on his face. He gestured for me to keep reading.

I scanned through more of the papers. As I read, I saw how advanced the plans were. There was a detailed outline for a school that would take in kids not thriving in the current educational system; a program of apprenticeships and work placements for children who'd gotten on the wrong side of the law; a mentoring program, placing kids with reformed criminals and showing them there was a way to avoid getting sucked back into the criminal world. It sounded amazing, and what was more, funding was in place to get the charity started. Lonnie had set aside a million pounds a year to make this happen. I was impressed.

Lonnie encouraged me to keep turning the pages. As I did so, I saw his ambitions didn't stop at one location. He had plans for a dozen of these projects. That would need some serious investment.

"Were you planning on using the stolen gold to finance this?" I placed the paperwork back in the box.

Lonnie shrugged and shot me a sly smile.

"I know you have the gold hidden somewhere. I don't approve of the way you got it, but what you'd planned to do with it is incredible. Do you still want this to happen? Is that why you're here?"

Lonnie nodded but then wrapped his hands around his throat and mimed being strangled.

"And you also think your death wasn't by natural causes."

He nodded before his gaze shifted to the plans for the charity.

"I'm not sure how much help I can be with setting up the charity," I said. "If the gold is hidden, it'll be of no use to anyone. And the police want it back."

Lonnie pressed a finger to his lips.

"I can't promise I'm not going to tell the police if I find out anything useful." I wasn't going to let Lonnie know I was helping Gunner, but he must know I'd have to report any gold bar discovered.

Lonnie dropped to his knees and held his hands together in a prayer position.

"I know this means a lot to you, and you don't want your family getting into trouble. I also see how great this charity could be, but it would be founded on crime. Is that right? What if the children who benefited from this work discovered their second chance came about because you stole?"

Lonnie leaned his head forward and rested it on my knees, sending a shard of ice cold through my veins as he made contact with me. He shot up and over to the pictures of his family, presenting them to me one at a time.

I sighed as I tried to ignore the sliver of uncertainty inside me. Stealing was wrong, and there was no way Lonnie could argue about that. But he'd done it for a noble cause, to help not only his family but to support thousands of troubled kids who didn't have anyone to turn to.

I placed the box back in the drawer, but it wouldn't lay flat so I couldn't get it closed. I pushed a little harder, but it refused to budge.

Taking the box out, I pushed my hand inside and felt around, expecting to feel a pen or piece of card stopping the box going back inside. What I felt instead was a small piece of rough wood raised slightly on the side of the drawer.

Shivers flooded down my spine as Lonnie shot to my side and waved his hands in front of me.

I looked up, expecting him to be alerting me to someone coming into the room or that Elita was waking up. No one came in, and Elita's snores floated around the study, confirming she wasn't going to bother me.

I returned to my investigation, prodding the wood and trying to get it to sit flat, but it was stuck in place. I gave it a thump with the side of my hand and heard the click of a latch opening.

Lonnie's gaze turned panicked. He hovered in front of me as if trying to block my way. He was hiding something. Something he didn't want me to see.

I dodged around him, but he blocked my path again. "What's the matter with you? I told you we need to be honest with each other if I'm going to help figure out who killed you."

Every time I tried to dodge around Lonnie, he kept getting in my way.

I stopped trying to run around him and glared at him, my hands on my hips. "You do realize you're a ghost? I can walk straight through you." Not that I wanted to. Whenever I walked through a ghost, it left me cold for days. It was as if they sucked some of the life out of me and gave me a shove toward the limbo afterlife they existed in. It wasn't a place I ever wanted to visit.

Lonnie's shoulders slumped before he stepped to one side and gestured me forward.

I walked slowly around the desk. The clicking sound had come from the other side. I carried on my investigation of the desk, creeping my fingers around the edge until I reached the front and discovered a small gap.

I pushed my fingers inside and felt something cold and smooth.

My heart sped up as I continued to feel around inside the gap. I'd never felt a gold bar before, but if I had, it would feel like this. I was certain of that.

I looked at Lonnie, who was peering anxiously at me. "Is this where you've been hiding your gold?"

Chapter 13

"Gold!" Elita sat up with a start, blinking her eyes and looking around the study. "Did you say something about gold?"

I spun around and concealed the desk compartment containing the gold bars. "No! I didn't say anything."

Elita's brow furrowed. "I heard you talking."

"I might have been muttering to myself. I have a habit of doing that." I looked at Flipper. "Or talking to my dog."

She smoothed her hair and gave a slight nod. "I was dreaming about Lonnie. He was telling me where he'd hidden the gold."

"Oh! Did he give you any useful clues?"

"No, it was just a dream. It didn't make any real sense." Elita slipped her feet into a pair of fluffy black slippers sitting on the floor by the sofa. "You still want to work here? No change of heart since last night?"

"I definitely do. I'm staying put."

She gave me a sharp look. "Why would you do that now you know we're criminals?"

"Because you aren't criminals anymore," I said. "At least, I don't think you are. It sounds as if Lonnie pursued a criminal lifestyle in order to provide for everyone else."

Elita sighed and stretched her arms over her head. "He didn't do anything for the greater good to begin with. He was a rogue. Then things changed."

"What happened to make Lonnie change?"

"I like to think that I had something to do with it," Elita said. "And, as you may have noticed, we don't have any children. There's no one to inherit the family name and take over the business."

I hadn't noticed that. I'd been too busy worrying about my own safety and whether there was a killer loose in the house. "You never had a family?"

"We tried for children." She played with a button on her bright red blouse. "For years, and we had a lot of fun trying. It never happened."

"I'm sorry to hear that."

Elita shrugged. "Lonnie was the reason it couldn't happen, not that he'd ever admit that."

Lonnie zoomed to Elita's side and shook his head. It looked like he still wasn't prepared to accept it.

"Lonnie wasn't fertile?" That question earned me an evil glare from him before he shot away from Elita.

"I had all the tests done, including spending a month in America having some specialist prod at me, only to tell me what I already knew. I was fit and healthy and able to have children. When they did the same to Lonnie, the results showed he didn't have any healthy swimmers. He wouldn't believe it and kept thinking he could defy the odds and all the medical knowledge under the sun, and still have a family."

"Male pride is a strange thing," I said.

"It's also a stupid thing," Elita said. "What was worse, when I got past childbearing age, he decided he needed a younger model, someone who would give him children. As if that made any difference."

"So, he left you for Chelsea."

Elita nodded, her lips pinching together. "It didn't happen with Chelsea either. And I know Lonnie was getting frustrated about that."

"Is that why he was interested in setting up the charity for troubled kids?" I asked. "It was his way of supporting and raising children who didn't have a good family to rely upon."

Her groomed eyebrows shot up. "How do you know about that?"

I looked back at the desk. "I was looking for some blank paper and found a file all about it. It sounds amazing."

"It was going to be one-of-a-kind." Elita sat back on the sofa. "Lonnie was so passionate about it. I was as well. We wanted to offer a place for children who didn't have a good start in life and were heading down the wrong path, just like some of the Cornells have in the past."

I smiled and waited for her to continue.

"We wanted to give them another option, and, in a way, create our own extended family and have the children we were never able to." She brushed a finger across her cheek. "Lonnie would have been an amazing father. He'd have loved those kids as if they were his own."

I looked over to see Lonnie skulking by the desk, a scowl on his face. Men and their egos.

"Why isn't the charity happening now?" I asked.

"Because I need the money to make it work," Elita said. "That was always Lonnie's big plan; secure enough money to make sure the charity would happen. Now the gold has gone, and so has Lonnie. Unless we decide to pull off another gold heist, the charity will remain a dream. One that died along with my cheating ex-husband."

"You could sell this place and move into somewhere smaller." I looked around at the expensive furnishings. The house must be worth a good few million.

"It wouldn't be enough," Elita said. "And we need a regular cash flow. You don't get rich helping troubled kids."

The gold bars hidden in the desk felt like they were alive, waiting to see if I'd reveal their whereabouts and help the poor unloved children. "Any ideas where Lonnie might have hidden the gold?"

Elita leaned forward. "Why the interest? Are you thinking you might run off with some of it?"

I stood up straight. "I don't steal from my employer."

"Make sure you don't," she said. "I'm not above setting you right if you double-cross this family. I'll protect them until the last breath has left my body."

I swallowed, noticing the steely glint in Elita's eyes. She was a gangster's wife through and through. "You have nothing to worry about. I'll do the job you need me to do and that's it." That and try to solve her ex-husband's murder.

Her face softened. "I do trust you. And I follow my gut instinct when I meet a person. It has never let me down. You and Helen are good girls."

I had to agree with that. Although being called a girl when I was closer to thirty than twenty was pushing it a bit.

"Well, I need to get ready for my date." Elita stood from the sofa. "Since I'm no longer a gangster's wife, I need to relax and have fun. Threatening the staff is something I'll let Michael do."

I chuckled awkwardly. "Let's hope it never comes to that."

"I couldn't agree more."

I was keen to change the subject. "Are you dating someone special?"

She winked at me. "Don't they always like to think they're the special one?"

I grinned. "I hope he's taking you somewhere nice."

"I'll be going to my favorite place." Elita raised her hand before leaving the study.

I glanced at Lonnie, who was still sulking by the desk. "Stop being so childish and help me figure out who killed you and who is after the gold." I jabbed a finger at the desk.

Lonnie glowered at me and vanished. So much for getting any help from him.

I slid the wood back into place over the hole in the desk, making sure no one else would stumble across my find. I was still undecided about what to do about this discovery. Gunner would kill to get his hands on evidence like this, but if I let him in on the find now, I'd never get a chance to figure out who killed Lonnie. Although, from the way he'd just been behaving, I wasn't sure he deserved any help. Stubborn, annoying ghost.

Still, I had something more urgent to investigate. Who was Elita now dating, and what would he be prepared to do to get Lonnie out of the way and himself into her arms?

***

I did a speedy tidy of the desk, made sure the box was back where it should be, and then dashed upstairs with Flipper.

My room looked out over the driveway so I had the perfect view for when Elita's suitor arrived for their date.

I settled on the window seat, Flipper resting his head on my knee, and waited.

Half an hour later, I was bored. No one had arrived, and Elita hadn't left in a car. Maybe they were running late or had decided not to pick up Elita. I pitied any man who stood Elita up. He'd end up with no knee caps and concrete shoes for committing such a crime.

There was a knock on my bedroom door, and I turned, trying to make myself look as innocent as possible and not like I was spying on my employer. "Come in."

Helen poked her head around the door. "You finished for the day?"

I let out a relieved sigh and gestured her to the window. "I'm waiting for Elita's boyfriend to arrive."

Her eyes widened, and she dashed over. "Who is it?"

"Elita didn't tell me. She let slip she's seeing someone. I want to know who."

"Someone who might want the criminal ex-husband out the way?" Helen peered out the window.

"That's what I was thinking," I said. "But he's a no-show."

"Maybe Elita and her new man worked together to get rid of Lonnie."

"That's possible," I said. "And I found damning evidence that puts Lonnie in the middle of the gold heist."

"What did you find?"

"Gold bars."

She opened her mouth. "Wow! That's some evidence. Have you told Gunner?"

"Not yet. I want to help Lonnie first."

Helen grabbed my arm. "Gunner needs to know about this."

"Since when have you been so interested in helping Gunner? I thought he was a thorn in your side, sent to cause you misery at every opportunity."

"He's all of that." Her cheeks glowed. "This gold will help him solve a huge case."

"But Lonnie's dead," I said. "Aren't we better focusing on finding his killer first? Then Gunner can come in, swoop up anyone who helped Lonnie steal the gold, and show you what a hot hero he is."

"He's not hot," she muttered.

"He's a little bit hot." My grin only widened when Helen refused to comment. "Let's go downstairs and see what Elita's up to. I might have missed her date arriving."

We worked our way through the downstairs rooms, looking for Elita and her mystery man.

Helen stopped by the back door. "I can hear voices outside."

I hurried to join her and tilted my head. "It's Elita. She must be having her date here. She said she was going to her favorite place. This must be it."

"We can't see anything from here."

"If we skirt around the edge of the garden, we can hide behind those bushes." I pointed to the large bushes shaped like hares. "We'll be able to see who Elita's with without being spotted."

We scuttled around the side of the house, being sure to stay out of sight of Elita and her mystery man.

I kept running through cold spots and slowed. It felt like I was running straight through ghosts, but I couldn't see any of them. Whatever it was, it felt odd.

"Hurry up!" Helen whispered.

Ignoring the feelings, I sped along. It took about five minutes to dash past the flower beds, but we were soon hidden by the giant green hares.

I settled on my knees and spotted a gap in the hedge. It gave me a good view of the terrace Elita was sitting on. She had a glass in one hand and wore a fitted cream silk dress, her dark hair pinned on top of her head.

"Who's she with?" Helen asked. "I don't see anybody else."

"Neither do I." I waited a moment to see if anyone would come out of the house, but other than Michael standing guard by the door, no one was around. She couldn't be having a date with herself.

Elita's laughter drifted toward me as she raised her glass at Michael. He nodded at her, and then slid his own glass out and took a swift sip before it vanished from sight.

I groaned and clamped my hand over my mouth. I was such an idiot.

"What did you see?" Helen shoved aside some leaves. "I can only see Elita's legs from here."

"It's Michael! She's dating the muscle."

Helen peered through the bush. "How can you tell?"

"I saw him with a drink. And she's talking to him. It makes sense now why he's so protective of her. He's not doing it because he's getting paid. He's doing it because he's into her."

"They could just be passing the time until her real date arrives."

Elita stood from her seat, looked around, and then pressed a gentle kiss to Michael's cheek.

I shook my head. "You don't kiss someone you're just passing the time with."

"Elita's got herself a hot younger lover," Helen said. "Good for her."

"Not so much for Lonnie. Michael was perfectly placed to sneak into Lonnie's private bathroom and kill him," I said.

We'd not only discovered who Elita's hot younger lover was but also a hot new suspect. Unfortunately, that suspect came with some serious muscles he wasn't afraid to use and, most likely, a fair few deadly weapons.

I was going to have to be careful dealing with Michael.

Chapter 14

I'd been waiting in the study for Elita to arrive for an hour. I'd done the few pieces of admin I could find, but needed her to tell me what to focus upon next.

I finished my mug of tea and was about to go in search of her when the study door opened and Elita wandered in, still in her silky nightie, which was covered by a long wine colored robe.

"Lorna! I'm sorry to have kept you." She rubbed the sleep from her eyes and yawned. "I meant to say yesterday that you can have this morning off. I was planning to have a late night."

"Your date went well?"

Elita smiled. "It was lovely. He's such a sweetie. You wouldn't think it to look at him, but he has a heart of gold and always wants to make me happy."

"How did you meet?" I was digging but wanted to see how open Elita would be when it came to her relationship with Michael.

She waved a hand in the air. "Through work connections."

At least she was being honest about that. "Is it serious?"

"I hope so." Elita looked around the study. "It would be nice to be with a man I know isn't doing things he shouldn't behind my back."

I was about to ask another question, but she raised her hand. "Enough chatter. I believe you have your own man. It doesn't pay to ignore them. Their egos don't like it. Why don't you go play with him for the morning? I bet you've been missing him."

"I have." Although I trusted Zach. He'd never get a wandering eye because I hadn't seen him for a couple of days. "If you're sure there's nothing you need me for, a morning off would be great."

"There's plenty of work to do, but nothing that can't wait," Elita said. "I'm grabbing the morning newspapers, a croissant, and heading back to bed. You're no use to me this morning. Go enjoy yourself."

"Any chance I can have the car back?" I asked. "I need it to visit Zach."

"Borrow the limo," Elita said. "Frankie will be outside somewhere. He'll take you where you need to go. Tell him I said it was okay for you to use the car."

It wasn't quite the answer I'd hoped for, but the idea of a limo ride sounded fun.

After sending Zach a quick text message to let him know I was on my way to our new house, I hurried outside with Flipper and discovered Frankie polishing the bumper of a black limousine. "I hope you don't mind giving me a lift."

Frankie pushed his black cap back. "Where are we going?"

I gave him the address of my new house.

"That's quite some drive," Frankie said. "It'll take about an hour to get there."

"Elita said it was okay for you to take me anywhere."

"It's not a problem," he said. "And the family hasn't got me booked in for any collections. Give me five minutes, and I'm all yours." He loped away across the driveway, leaving Flipper and me waiting by the limousine.

Frankie returned with a thermos flask and a lunchbox. "I might as well make the most of the journey. I never know how long I'll be waiting around. I hate getting hungry."

Frankie's smile was warm enough, but it didn't reach his eyes. "That's fine by me. It must get boring having to wait for people."

"I'm used to it." He opened the back door for me, and I clambered in, along with Flipper. He walked around to the driver's door and climbed in. "And I don't mind. They pay well, and I often get a few perks thrown in, especially if I've had to wait around late at night."

"What kind of perks?" I asked as Frankie smoothly manoeuvred the limousine along the driveway and onto the main road.

"This and that." His gaze met mine for a second in the rear-view mirror. "You know what business the Cornells are in?"

"I'm getting an idea," I said.

"Best to keep that idea to yourself," he said. "The family doesn't like people talking."

I took that as a hint to keep my mouth shut, sat back in the expensive leather seat, and let Frankie concentrate on his driving.

As I watched the countryside roll past, I realized the suspects were piling up when it came to Lonnie and who'd killed him.

I wasn't ready to rule out Elita, even though she seemed to care for him. I didn't know Chelsea well enough, but she had a great motive, and she was interested in information about the gold, which suggested she had plans for taking it. Then there was Michael and his relationship with Elita. If they'd gotten together when Lonnie was still on the scene, it wouldn't have been approved of. Michael could have decided to get revenge on Elita's behalf. I wasn't sure how deep his loyalties ran and to which family members it extended.

And what about Ignatius, the older brother? He had an evil side, and I wouldn't put it past him to think it acceptable to get rid of his younger brother and remove an obstacle.

And finally Carson, the sneaky right-hand man. Now Lonnie was gone, who was he loyal to? Had he started looking out for himself now his boss had gone or didn't he care who he reported to so long as the money kept coming in?

I mulled over the suspects as we drove through the Nottinghamshire countryside, heading toward the Peak District and my new house. Frankie made the occasional comment as we passed by certain landmarks, but other than that, he was happy to entertain himself by listening to the radio and humming under his breath.

The limo slowed, and I looked out the window to see we were almost there. "Just keep going. You'll see a new house on the left-hand side. It won't show up on your GPS yet."

Frankie nodded and did as instructed. He stopped the limousine and hopped out to open my door. "Any idea what time you'll be finished?"

"I'm not sure. I'll be a few hours."

"I'll go and find myself a nice spot then," he said. "I can eat and have a nap, unless you want me to keep watch for any reason."

I raised my eyebrows. "You don't need to keep watch over me. I'll be safe here."

Frankie shrugged as he shut the door and returned to his own seat. He leaned over and handed me a card. "Give this number a call when you're done. I'll collect you."

I gave him a wave as the limousine pulled away. Frankie was polite enough, but I'd begun to get paranoid toward the end of the ride that he was watching me. I couldn't figure out why, though, unless I needed to add him to the suspect list, as well. The chauffeur did it. It sounded like something out of an Agatha Christie novel.

I shook my head. I needed to focus on the family first. If none of them proved fruitful, I'd move onto members of staff.

Flipper gave a happy bark and bounded away from me. I turned and saw his object of affection. Jessie was running toward him with equal speed, letting out her own happy barks as they almost collided and then danced around each other, their tails up as they sniffed a greeting.

Zach emerged from around the side of the house a few seconds later, a smile spreading across his face as he spotted me.

I took a step back, admiring the way Zach so easily pulled off the dusty builder look. I was used to seeing him in grass stained pants with dirt under his nails, but the rugged builder look was a good fit for him as well.

He grabbed hold of me and gave me a kiss. "This is a great surprise."

"A boss with a hangover has its advantages," I said. "Plus, she let me borrow the limousine for the morning. I'm all yours."

He took hold of my hand and led me toward the house. "Don't be disappointed that all the fixtures and fittings aren't where they need to be. It's getting there."

"I already love it," I said. Zach had been sending pictures and updates on the progress of the house ever since he'd gotten started. Although I'd only gotten to visit a few times in the last month, I was so proud of what he was achieving and how beautiful our home was going to be when it was finished.

"The kitchen units arrived yesterday," he said. "I'm focusing on that for the next couple of weeks. After that's in and the bathrooms are done, all that's left is the painting and papering."

"Then we can move in." I stood on my tiptoes and planted a kiss on his cheek. "It's going to be such an amazing home."

"It is." Zach grinned down at me. "And it's all ours."

"Well, ours, the dogs, Helen's, and Gunner's."

"Speaking of which, Gunner's out on a wood run," Zach said. "We've run out of timber. He'll be back soon. He wants to talk to you about how things are going at the Cornell house."

I pretended to admire the new front door, tapping my fingers against the wood and inspecting the brass fittings.

Zach's hand tightened on my waist. "How is it going?"

"The ghost isn't causing any problems," I said.

"And the rest of the family? The ones who are alive? The ones who are criminals?"

"Most of them are behaving themselves." I kept my gaze on the door. I was never a good liar.

"And which ones aren't behaving themselves?"

"Stop worrying about me," I said. "As you can see, I'm here and I'm fine. I'd let you know if anything serious was happening." The fact I knew where several gold bars were hidden played on my mind, but I couldn't tell Zach. He wouldn't let me keep that information a secret so I could help a ghost.

"Just don't go taking any foolish risks," Zach said.

"As if I would."

"As if you wouldn't."

"Come on. Show me around our gorgeous house."

Zach grumbled under his breath for a few seconds before guiding me around the side of the house. All the windows were installed, and I could see how beautiful the finished house would look.

"This is the temporary entrance into the kitchen. It'll be bricked in soon." Zach opened the door, and I walked through in front of him. There wasn't much to see, other than cables hanging out the wall and a concrete floor.

I was drawn to the large double doors. The views were stunning. All I could see for miles were trees, fields, and the occasional herd of cows. I could feel the tension leaving my shoulders as I admired the view.

"Just think, every morning, we can wake up and look at that." Zach stood behind me and placed his hands on my shoulders.

"I can't think of anything I'd like more," I said.

"Wait until you see the view from the bathroom," Zach said. "You're never going to want to get out of the bath."

The dogs ran through the kitchen, play chasing each other, and we followed them as Zach showed me our new dining room, the lounge, study, and a games room.

"I thought we hadn't decided what this was going to be." I looked around the empty shell of the room that was being called a games room.

"Gunner pestered me so much that I gave in," Zach said. "He said he'd need somewhere to get away from all the girly stuff that's bound to fill the house."

"That girly stuff won't be mine," I said.

"He wasn't referring to you." Zach grinned. "I don't suppose Helen has revealed she's madly in love with my brother yet, has she?"

"The last time I spoke to her about him she went red and got flustered. I see that as a positive sign."

"Those two need to sort themselves out," Zach said.

I turned as I caught a glimpse of movement out the corner of one eye. I could hear the dogs close by and assumed it must be them still playing. Whenever they were together, they ended up getting into mischief and making a lot of noise doing it.

The sound of a vehicle reversing into the driveway caught my attention.

"That must be Gunner." Zach walked through the house and out the front door, and I followed him.

Gunner hopped out the cab of a white van, looking equally as dusty as Zach. He grinned when he spotted me. "I heard you were paying us a visit. What do you think of the place?"

"It's looking great," I said.

He dropped a quick kiss on my cheek. "Your boyfriend's been working me like a dog whenever he gets the opportunity. This is supposed to be my day off from my real job, but as soon as Zach heard I had free time, that was it. I had to get over here and start hammering walls and running around like his skivvy."

"He volunteered to come here," Zach said.

"I promise you, Zach's got me here under pain of torture." Gunner grinned at me again.

As much as he protested, I got the impression Gunner loved being here. He'd been without a permanent home for years, flitting from rented room to rented room as his job took him around the country. A recent work promotion meant he had a permanent base with the police and could put down roots. He'd decided to do that with us.

I didn't mind. Gunner was fun to be around, and the brothers got on well. How he handled Helen was another matter, but I'd leave them to figure that out.

"So, how's the undercover work going with the Cornells?" Although Gunner's grin remained, his gaze grew serious.

"Not much to report, so far." I kicked a loose stone along the ground.

"Lorna's only been at the house five minutes," Zach said. "You don't want her getting spotted snooping."

Gunner raised a hand. "The Cornells are a big deal. If we take them down, it'll be incredible. There's a list of crimes linked to this family longer than both my arms."

"Lorna said she'd help you, and she will," Zach said. "Give her a chance to earn their trust before you put a wire on her and get her to interrogate the entire household."

I placed a hand on Zach's arm. "It's fine. And I am having a look around to see if I can find anything useful. Like Zach said, it's early days. I won't uncover their deep dark secrets right away." I ignored the image of a gold bar that flashed through my thoughts. I would tell Gunner about the gold as soon as I'd helped Lonnie.

"We're still interested in the gold robbery the Cornells are implicated in," Gunner said.

I swallowed my nerves. It was as if he'd read my mind. "I imagine you are. How much did they steal again?"

"Twenty-five million," Gunner said. "And none of it has ever been discovered. We assumed they were shipping the gold to another country or had an agent here, who was slowly melting the gold and selling it off under our noses."

"I don't think the family will leave gold bars lying around for me to find," I said, hoping my lie wasn't too easy to see through. "If I hear any useful information, I'll pass it on."

"Look through their paperwork," Gunner said. "A paper trail is the best we can hope for if the gold has gone. There must be something to stick this crime to the family. Also, see if you can find anything about dodgy businesses they're running."

"What would I need to find to make me think the business is dodgy?"

"Strange tax returns or large injections of cash that aren't easy to explain."

"I haven't seen anything like that," I said. "I've been working on getting the admin sorted after Lonnie's funeral."

"And as I keep saying," Zach muttered, "Lorna doesn't want to take any unnecessary risks by pushing too hard."

"It's important we have this information." Gunner's grin faded.

"I'll get you what I can," I said. I looked at the glower on Zach's face. "While keeping myself super safe."

Gunner ran a hand through his dusty hair. "Anything you can get will be good. The Cornell family is still active in the criminal underworld and well-connected. If we remove them from the equation, it'll bring down other networks. A lot of innocent people will be spared intimidation with the Cornells out of the picture."

I gritted my teeth. It was as if Gunner was trying to guilt me into declaring what I knew.

"Enough talk of criminals," Zach said. "I was going to show Lorna what we've been doing upstairs."

Gunner's grin returned. "You don't want me interfering if you're taking your lady upstairs."

I smacked his arm. "Looking at empty bedrooms is not my idea of a romantic time."

"I don't know. The place has a certain romantic charm to it." Gunner followed us into the house. "How's the lovely Helen? I hope she's not being too irritating around the family, or she might discover they want to take her for a long walk along a short pier."

"Helen's being her usual charming self," I said. "The family adores her."

"Is she seeing anyone?" Gunner scuffed his work boot along the floor. "I know she likes the posh types. I imagine the Cornells aren't for her. There is money in that family, so I just wondered..."

"If you're asking if she's still single and interested in you, I really can't comment," I said. "No one in the family has caught Helen's eye yet. That doesn't mean she isn't looking."

"Helen's a sensible lady. She'll know not to get involved with anybody in that family," Gunner said.

"I don't know about that," I said, not able to resist teasing just a little. "Lonnie's older brother was paying Helen attention when we had a party, and Lonnie's ex-wife is keen on getting him set up."

"You mean Ignatius Cornell!" Gunner frowned and shook his head. "Don't mess with him."

"I got the impression he'd quite like to mess around with Helen."

Gunner grabbed hold of my arm. "I'm being serious. Get on the wrong side of him and you're history. I've got his name against half a dozen murders. You don't play with him and get away with it. Tell Helen to steer clear. You too."

The intense look in Gunner's eyes made me realize he wasn't joking. "Murder? I didn't think that was what the family was into."

Gunner sighed. "Just Ignatius. He has trouble controlling his temper. He likes his violence messy. Lonnie was the brains in the family. Hee planned the robberies and crimes involving blackmail and extortion. And he was good at making sure he never left evidence behind."

"Okay. I'll tell Helen to avoid Ignatius," I said.

"You avoid him too," Zach said. "And no more trying to get information out of Ignatius so my idiot brother can solve a crime. He's smart enough to do that for himself."

I gulped. Messy violence and murder. This was more serious than stolen gold. What had I gotten myself into?

Chapter 15

Three hours later, I'd viewed every room in the house twice and helped Zach unpack our new kitchen units ready to be installed.

It was nice to get involved with doing something on the house, even though it was only unpacking boxes and looking at designs for the kitchen. Every time I came here, I realized how excited I was about starting this part of my life with Zach.

I stood outside the front of the house, having sent a message to Frankie telling him I was ready to be picked up.

Flipper kept looking back at the house and gently whining.

I gave his head a pat. "I know. We both miss Jessie and Zach. We'll be with them soon enough."

Flipper looked up at me and whined again.

"It's not that bad. If you want, I can set up a Skype call so you can see Jessie."

Flipper covered his nose with one paw. He didn't think much of that idea. I felt the same. A Skype call wasn't the same as a snuggle and sharing a meal with the one you love.

The limousine pulled up beside me, and Frankie rolled down the window. "Ready to go home?"

I nodded and let myself into the back, Flipper jumping in in front of me.

"Did you have a good time?" Frankie asked as he cruised away from the house.

"I did," I said. "I'm going to be moving in soon."

Frankie's gaze was on mine in the rear-view mirror. "It's a nice place. You buying alone?"

"No, I'm moving in with a few friends," I said, "including Helen. You might have seen her around the house."

"The curvy blonde with the high heels?"

I had to smile at that description. Trust Frankie to notice those things first. "That's the one."

"I suppose she's taken?" he asked

"In a way," I said.

Frankie shrugged. "And you?"

"I'm definitely taken," I said. It was time for a change of topic. "What did you get up to while you were waiting for me?"

"This and that."

I shook my head and looked out the window. If he wanted to behave like a man of mystery that was fine by me. After my time walking around the house, I was feeling sleepy and relaxed back into the seat.

Flipper nestled his head on my lap, also seeming to think a nap would be a good idea.

My eyes had only been closed for a few minutes before I felt the limousine slow. "Is something wrong?"

"Nothing's wrong." Frankie glanced at me. "I just need to take care of a bit of business."

The privacy shield slid up, hiding me from Frankie's view. I sat up swiftly in my seat. What was he doing?

The passenger door opened, and Ignatius Cornell climbed in.

I sucked in a breath, ignoring the thrumming of my nerves. "I didn't realize we were picking you up on the way to the house." If I had, I'd have made other arrangements. Spending any time in an enclosed space with Ignatius wasn't something I relished.

Ignatius tapped a knuckle on the privacy screen. The limousine started to move. He turned and looked at me in silence, his forehead wrinkled and his eyes narrowed.

"Have you been out somewhere nice?" I asked as an uncomfortable trickle of fear slid down my spine.

"I wouldn't say nice," Ignatius said. He ignored Flipper who sniffed his hands.

"Business?"

Ignatius nodded. "What have you been doing this morning?"

His cold tone made me realize he wasn't asking to be sociable. "Personal business."

"Such as?"

"Such as it's personal," I said. "Why do you need to know what I'm doing on my morning off?"

"Because Elita has grown soft," he said. "She barely knows you, but she's letting you out of the house on your own and using the family vehicles."

"If I'd have known borrowing the limousine was going to cause you difficulty, I wouldn't have done it," I said.

"The car isn't the issue. Elita should know better. She trusts too easily, though, and has always worn her heart on her sleeve. And she's never able to keep quiet about things."

"Why wouldn't she trust me?"

"I haven't forgotten your friend is involved with a cop."

"They're not involved," I said. "And he's a decent guy."

"No one decent ever works for the police," Ignatius said. "Most of them are bent, anyway."

"How would you know that?"

"Because I'm the one who bends them." Ignatius shot me a smug smile. "What's the name of your policeman friend?"

There was no way I was going to tell him anything about Gunner. "Helen's not involved with a police officer. Even if she is, she wouldn't let it affect her work for the family."

Ignatius adjusted the collar on his white shirt. "What's your background?"

"My work background?" I blinked at him. "Just ask Elita. She has everything about my work history and experience."

"Not the official information you put out to the public," Ignatius said. "Where were you born? Who is your family? Where did you go to school? Who do you know?"

"None of that is relevant to my work with you." My hands were clenched, and I forced myself to relax. This guy was creeping me out even more than usual.

Ignatius's eyes narrowed. "It's all relevant if it impacts the family."

"It won't," I said. "I grew up in an ordinary family and went to a normal school. I didn't go to a secret spy school if that's what you're trying to figure out."

He snorted. "You'd make a terrible spy. Your emotions are written all over your face."

I frowned. "So, you can tell I'm uncomfortable that you've hitched a ride with me."

"You have nothing to worry about," Ignatius said, "for now."

"Meaning?" I shifted in my seat, and my gaze went to the door handle. I bet Frankie had locked it. It would be stupid to try to get out of a moving vehicle, but that didn't mean I wasn't tempted.

"Mom tells me you see ghosts."

I tried not to show my surprise. "Why would she tell you that?"

"She reckons she sees them too," Ignatius said. "It's not so strange in our family. People get these weird vibes and feelings. I have them."

This had my interest. "You can see ghosts?"

Ignatius shrugged. "I didn't say that. What do you see?"

"I don't see anything," I said.

"When you lie, your bottom lip trembles," Ignatius said, his gaze on my mouth. "It's your tell. Everyone has one."

I squeezed my lips together. "I haven't got a clue what you're talking about."

"You can be straight with me," he said. "I won't think you're weird if you tell me you can see ghosts."

"That's hardly comforting," I said. "What makes you think your mom can see ghosts?"

"The things she says are too accurate to be a coincidence. And she's always gazing into the distance as if she can see something the rest of us can't. My great grandmother had the same gift. Some people called her a witch. I think she was just clever at reading people, seeing the little facial tics and gestures that gave away their secrets."

"Like you spotting my bottom lip shaking?"

Ignatius smiled. "Exactly like that. So, since you can see ghosts, have you seen any around the house?"

"No."

He tipped his head back, his gaze remaining on me. "Seen Lonnie?"

"If I had, what do you think he'd be telling me about you?" I tried to appear nonchalant as I looked out the tinted window.

"He'd tell you to be careful," Ignatius said, shifting closer to me. "He would also tell you not to say anything about the gold and where it's hidden."

"Which suggests he doesn't trust you," I said. "If he's hiding this gold from you, then he must think you want to do something bad with it."

"Not something bad," Ignatius said. "But I don't want to spend it on all those ruined kids."

"Lonnie's charity sounds good. Why would you want to take that away?" I asked. "Don't you want to carry on his legacy?"

"The man was a deluded fool," Ignatius said. "Once you're in this life, you don't get out. Why would you want to? You have everything you need, including the respect of others."

"If you get that respect by frightening and hurting other people, is that right?"

"That's the way things are done," Ignatius said. "Lonnie knew that. He was a fool for trying to change things."

"Fool enough for you to want him out of your way?" It was a dangerous question to ask, but I couldn't avoid it.

Ignatius grabbed my hand, and Flipper raised his head and growled.

He shot a sharp glare at Flipper. "Keep your dog away from me if you don't want him hurt."

"I've trained him to attack," I said. "He won't hesitate to bite you if he thinks you're going to harm me."

Ignatius dropped his tight hold on my hand. "I'd never kill Lonnie. Although, I wanted to more than once."

"What stopped you?" I tried to keep my voice as even as possible, even though my heart lurched in my chest.

"He was my brother," Ignatius said. "He was an idiot and soft in the head, but I still loved him. And he was family. You don't destroy family. There are plenty of other targets to focus upon. People to make vanish."

"You must have been frustrated about the gold, though," I said. "If he kept it hidden from you, why not try to find it? Perhaps you went to talk to Lonnie when he was in the bath and he refused to help you. You got mad and lashed out at him."

"It didn't happen like that," Ignatius said.

"How did it happen?" I asked. "Supposing I can see Lonnie's ghost and he's telling me his death wasn't an accident. Why shouldn't you be the top suspect?"

"Because we're family!" Ignatius raised his hands skyward as if that statement solved everything.

That wasn't a good enough reason to remove him as a suspect, but I didn't know how much farther to push Ignatius. I was walking a dangerous line by asking these questions and had promised Zach I wouldn't put myself in harm's way. Looking at the deadly glare Ignatius was giving me, I'd done just that.

"Lonnie should have known better," Ignatius said. "He should look after family first."

"You look very well cared for," I said.

"The material things aren't an issue." He sat back in his seat. "It's always family first. Nothing else beats that."

"Perhaps Lonnie no longer thought that, since he wouldn't share the location of the gold with you."

"Has he told you something?" Ignatius's gaze lasered in on me. "I have a right to know."

"I don't know where all the gold is," I said. Well, I knew where a couple of bars were, so technically, I wasn't lying.

"You'd tell me if Lonnie had revealed anything to you?" Ignatius shoved a hand inside his jacket.

I slid away, taking Flipper with me. What if Ignatius pulled out a gun?

"Relax." He smirked as he opened his wallet and took out some money. "I thought you might like an... incentive to help you remember."

The muscles in my neck cracked with tension. "Money won't help me remember anything. And I haven't even confirmed that I can see Lonnie's ghost. If you get these weird vibes, maybe you could see him yourself if you looked hard enough. Why don't you ask him what happened to the gold?"

Ignatius stuffed his wallet away and huffed loudly. "I don't see him."

"Your mom said she can see him. Get her to ask Lonnie what's going on. There's no reason for him to keep the location of the gold a secret from her."

"Mom would probably give it all away to the nearest orphanage." Ignatius shook his head. "I'll give you a day to remember everything you know about the missing gold."

I swallowed. "It won't help."

"It will. This is a family matter. You need to keep quiet about this."

"I'm not talking to anybody about the gold," I said. "Who would I tell?"

"Your friend's policeman boyfriend."

I pressed my lips together again, determined not to reveal the lie I was about to say. "I wouldn't do that. I barely know him."

"Make sure it stays that way," Ignatius said. "If I hear the police are sniffing around us, you're the first person I'll come looking for. I'll want to know who you've been flapping your gums to."

"I never flap my gums," I said.

He tapped on the privacy shield, and the limousine slowed. "I'm getting out here."

"More business to deal with?"

Ignatius shot me a glare. "Something like that. Take care of yourself, Lorna Shadow. And be careful about who you speak to. Word has a way of getting back to me. You won't like to see me when I'm unhappy."

I raised my eyebrows. If this was Ignatius being happy, I didn't want to see him with his grumpy head on.

Flipper growled at Ignatius as he slid off the seat and out the passenger door.

I petted Flipper's head as I calmed my breathing. I now had my top suspect in Lonnie's murder.

I just had to stay alive long enough to prove it was him.

Chapter 16

I spent a couple of hours working with Elita when I got back from my visit to our new house and my unpleasant encounter with Ignatius. My heart pounded every time I thought about the menacing words he'd left me with.

After I finished work, I hurried to the kitchen and discovered Helen standing at the stove, stirring a large pot of something smelling of basil and oregano.

"I thought we'd have Italian tonight," Helen said, "since it's in keeping with the family."

I slumped into a seat at the kitchen table.

"Hard day?" she asked.

I gave her a quick update about my visit to see Zach and my encounter with Ignatius afterward.

"Frankie must have tipped him off that I was alone," I said. "I thought he was giving me an odd look when I left the limo. Now, I know why."

"We need to keep away from Ignatius," Helen said. "I don't like the sound of his bullying one bit."

"It's difficult, though," I said. "When I saw Gunner, he was putting pressure on me to find out more. He wants to solve this gold robbery and put the Cornells away."

"I'm not having him bully you." Helen placed the spoon she was holding on the table and took out her phone, her fingers skimming across the keys. "There! That should stop him."

"What did you do?"

"I told Gunner to back off," she said. "He doesn't have the right to hassle you."

"Does anybody?" I grinned at her.

"I do, of course," Helen said. "And Zach might boss you around now and again if you're misbehaving too much. But Gunner, definitely not."

"I didn't know you had his private number."

Helen blushed and waved a hand in the air. "That's not the point. Let me know if he causes you any more trouble. I'll tell him off again."

"That'll solve all my worries. I know how much he hates you hassling him."

"I give as good as I get when it comes to Gunner Booth," she said. "His swagger doesn't fool me."

I was about to sample a piece of garlic bread Helen had placed on the table, when Lonnie shot into view, spinning around me several times and waving his hands in the air.

Flipper jumped up and chased Lonnie around the kitchen as he continued to career past furniture and bump into chairs.

Helen looked from me to Flipper. "I'm guessing from how pale you've gone and how weirdly Flipper's behaving that we've got company."

"Lonnie's here." I watched as he continued to spin around the kitchen, waving his hands, a look of distress on his face. "And something's not right with him."

Helen righted a kitchen chair Lonnie had knocked over. "What's the problem?"

"He's not looking happy."

Lonnie slowed by the kitchen back door and gestured toward it.

"He wants us to go outside." I looked longingly at the warm garlic bread.

"The bolognese can cook on its own for a while," Helen said. "Why don't we go see what our ghostly friend is worried about?"

I hopped up from my seat, and we hurried out the back door.

The second we got outside, I could hear raised female voices screeching at each other.

"That sounds bad," Helen said.

"That sounds like Elita and Chelsea fighting again." Lonnie nodded and beckoned us to hurry.

We ran past the tennis courts and over to the swimming pool. Elita and Chelsea stood almost nose to nose, glaring at each other. Michael, Ignatius, and Carson were also there.

We hid behind a large bush with Lonnie and Flipper and listened in to the argument.

"If you tell me again that I have to leave this house, I'll rip that weave right out of your scalp." Elita shoved Chelsea.

Chelsea staggered back on her high heels but righted herself and shoved back equally as hard. "No one wants you here. You're not welcome anymore."

"That's not true," Elita screeched. "Lonnie wouldn't want me on the streets."

"You're not going to be out on the streets, you dumb mare," Chelsea said. "Lonnie gave you more than your fair share when he divorced you and your saggy backside. He wouldn't want you here, knowing how much it upsets me."

"Ladies, you don't need to fight about this," Ignatius said. From the look of amusement on his face, he was enjoying watching them argue.

"She's not staying." Chelsea jabbed a finger at Elita. "I want her gone."

"The house is big enough for all of us." Carson gave a shrug and turned his attention to the drink in his hand.

"She's always sneaking around and watching me," Chelsea said.

"I'm the one sneaking! I caught you in my bedroom last week," Elita said. "What were you looking for?"

"The pearls you'd stolen from me," Chelsea said. "And don't even try to deny it. Lonnie gave them to me just before he died."

"Lonnie gives all his women jewelry," Ignatius said. "He most likely bought you identical necklaces so you wouldn't fight like this."

"He'd never do that." Chelsea sniffed and glared at Elita. "He told me they were one-of-a-kind."

"He'd do anything for a quiet life," Ignatius said. "My brother didn't like stress."

"I never stressed him out," Chelsea said. "I loved the man. I made him happy after years of having to put up with this worn out old tart."

"You loved him so much you couldn't even be bothered to arrange his funeral," Elita said.

"More like you shoved me out the way and did everything you wanted without bothering to ask me."

Michael cleared his throat. "It might be better if you have some time apart and cool off."

Chelsea waved a hand at Michael. "You keep out of this. I know you're on Elita's side."

"Michael is as much a part of the family as any of us," Elita said. "In fact, more so than you. You barely knew

Lonnie before you forced him to put a diamond on your finger. Michael has been here since he was a child."

"Shouldn't we do something?" Helen whispered.

"You want to get in the middle of a Cornell family fight?" I asked. "I don't fancy risking my neck over this."

Ignatius stepped forward and took hold of Chelsea's arm. "My dear, it might be a good idea if you go for a walk and calm down."

"I'm calm!" Chelsea shook his hand off. "It's this old crone who needs to sort herself out." She glared at Elita. "You've got a week, then I want you out of here."

Elita folded her arms over her chest. "I'm going nowhere."

"Neither am I," Chelsea said. "And I'm not living in this house with you."

"You're welcome to leave," Elita said. "I can have your bags packed for you. You can be out of here by the end of the day. It'll be my pleasure to arrange that."

"Like I'd ever leave here," Chelsea hissed. "The second I did, you'd change the locks to stop me from getting back in."

"That's a good idea." Elita smirked at Chelsea. "The next time you plan a girls' weekend away, I might have to do that."

Chelsea shrieked in rage and ran at Elita, knocking her backward and sending them both into the swimming pool.

"Now she's done it," Helen said.

I shook my head. "This isn't going to help them figure out their living arrangements."

Both women surfaced and gasped for air.

Flipper dashed away from the bush we'd been lurking behind and headed straight toward the pool.

"Flipper!" I said in a loud whisper, trying to stop him from revealing us.

He ignored me, bounded toward the swimming pool, and launched himself in, landing on top of Chelsea.

Lonnie pointed at the two women flailing about in the swimming pool.

"No way!" I shook my head. "I'm not getting involved in this fight. The men can deal with this."

Elita and Chelsea were screaming and flapping their arms.

Flipper had a hold of Chelsea's collar and was dragging her through the water.

I couldn't decide if he was helping her or trying to drown her. Whatever he was doing, it wasn't helping. Chelsea was screaming even louder.

"Maybe you should help," Helen said.

"Why me? I don't see you running to jump in the water," I said.

"I've just done my hair," she said. "And you, well, you haven't. You're also a better swimmer than me. I remember you got your five hundred meter swimming badge a year before I did."

I groaned. "Please don't make me do this."

Helen grinned. "I'd only get in the way if I tried to help. Then you'd have to rescue me too."

Michael was hovering by the pool's edge, holding his hand out to Elita. Why wasn't he going in and dragging her out?

Ignatius was bent over laughing and clutching his stomach, and Carson was ignoring it all. So much for men and their chivalry. Elita and Chelsea could be drowning, and the three of them were useless.

"For goodness sake!" I ran toward the pool. "Jump in and help!" I nudged Michael as I teetered on the edge, still not keen to launch myself into the water.

"I would, but I can't swim." Michael gave me an apologetic look. "Elita's not too good in the water either."

As if to prove that point, Elita shrieked and her head went under.

I looked over to where Ignatius was still doubled over laughing. "You help her."

"Not a chance," he spluttered. "I'm having too much fun watching. Hey, Carson, do you fancy placing a bet on who gets out alive?"

Carson didn't even bother to reply and refused to meet my gaze as I glared at him. He probably didn't want to ruin his designer suit by diving into the chlorinated water.

With an irritated sigh, I kicked off my shoes, took a deep breath and jumped in.

Chapter 17

I grabbed hold of Elita, hooked her around the arms and pulled her back to the surface.

She spat out water and started to scream the second she surfaced.

"Calm down," I said. "I've got you now. Hold onto me, and you'll be fine."

Elita coughed out water and turned her gaze to me. Her cheeks were smeared with mascara. "Lorna! Thanks heaven. I thought I was going to drown."

"I'll get you out of here," I said.

"What about Chelsea?" she asked, a hopeful glint in her eyes. "Did she make it?"

"Flipper's looking after her." I glanced over to see he'd dragged Chelsea to the side of the pool. She was clinging to the cdgc, looking as bedraggled as Elita. Maybe a dunk in a cold swimming pool would cool her temper.

I swam to the shallow end of the pool, towing Elita behind me. "You can put your feet down here."

Elita sank her legs down and let out a relieved sigh. "I'm so glad you're here. Those boys are worse than useless. You can't rely on a man for anything."

"You can't rely on that lot, that's for sure." I shot an angry glare at the three men who stood by the pool watching the action.

Michael hurried to the steps and held his hand out to Elita as we emerged from the water.

"Thank you, Michael," she said as she grabbed his hand.

"I'm sorry I couldn't come in and help." He removed his jacket and placed it around Elita's shoulders. "I can't swim."

"Then I'm going to pay for you to have lessons," Elita said. "I need you looking out for me at all times."

"Yes, of course." Michael dipped his head. "I'm sorry for letting you down."

Elita patted his arm before turning her attention to Chelsea, who was clambering out of the pool and shooing Flipper away. "She's determined to get me out of this house."

I wrung water out of my hair. "It seems like neither of you want to leave."

"It's as much mine as it is hers." Elita wiped some of the mascara off her face, and sank into a seat. "Lonnie wanted me to be comfortable."

Chelsea spun toward Elita, spattering Ignatius with water as she did so. "I'll be comfortable as soon as you get your scrawny backside out of here."

"No more fighting," I said. "It's not helping you figure out what to do about your living arrangements."

"Lonnie had this naive idea the two of them would become friends." Ignatius was still chuckling to himself. It made me want to shove him in the swimming pool and see how he liked it.

"That's never going to happen," Chelsea said. "This is my house now. I get to decide who stays here."

"Lonnie's will stated otherwise." Elita looked at her sodden clothing.

"If you have any love left for Lonnie, you'd leave this house and let me get on with my life," Chelsea said.

Elita glared at her. "Why would I do that?"

"Because he was my husband," Chelsea said. "He'd had his turn with you. You weren't good enough to keep him. I'm the real wife."

Elita lurched toward Chelsea, but Michael put a restraining hand on her arm. "She's not worth it," he muttered.

"There is a solution to this." Ignatius wiped his eyes, his laughter fading as he walked toward the edge of the swimming pool.

"What's that?" Chelsea asked.

"We find the hidden gold," Ignatius said. "If we have that, we can all buy houses on every continent and still have plenty left over."

"We've looked everywhere for it," Chelsea said, her tone sulky. "No one knows where the stupid gold is hidden."

"Lonnie does." Sylvia rolled herself onto the pool terrace.

Chelsea shook her head. "Crazy old woman. She doesn't even know her own son is dead."

"Show some respect, girl," Sylvia said. "I know what's going on here. And I see when someone is more interested in money than the man she married."

"That's not true!" Chelsea glared at Sylvia then ducked her head.

"He should have stayed with Elita," Sylvia said. "She has her faults, but family is important to her."

"Thank you, Sylvia." Elita tipped her head to one side. "Although, what are my faults?"

Sylvia shook her head. "The family keeps fighting over what Lonnie left behind. That needs to be resolved."

"Then ask Lonnie where the gold is," Ignatius said. "You're convinced he's still around and you can see him. Get him to tell us where he hid it, and the fighting will end. Some of us worked hard to make sure we got that gold. And now, we can't make use of it because Lonnie was an idiot."

"He was a smart boy," Sylvia said, "smart enough to know not to trust you with the location of the gold."

"I should leave you to it if you have family matters to discuss." I was torn between finding out more about the gold and hightailing it out of this house and forgetting I'd ever met Lonnie Cornell and this family.

"You're involved now." Sylvia fixed me with a steely gaze. "You can't leave until you've done what you need to."

"You mean the filing?" Chelsea's eyes narrowed.

"Exactly that." Elita flipped her sodden hair over one shoulder. "Now, Lorna, will you be a sweetie and give me a hand up?"

I did as instructed, and she pulled me closer so her mouth was by my ear. "Don't let Chelsea in on any information you have about the gold. She's not getting her scheming hands on it."

I pulled back and nodded.

"And you need to get changed after saving me from the pool." Elita grinned, walked past Chelsea, and shoved her back into the water.

Chelsea shrieked as she went under.

Flipper barked before jumping in, ever the brave hero. He was followed by Reggie, who gave a yip of delight, jumped off Sylvia's lap, and landed on Chelsea's head as he leaped into the pool.

I turn toward Helen, my shoulders shaking as I tried not to laugh as Chelsea screamed and spluttered as Flipper saved her for the second time.

"I'll kill her!" Chelsea waved away the offer of a towel from Ignatius. "She might have been the first Cornell wife, but that doesn't give her the right to push me around."

I noticed the lethal glint in Chelsea's eyes. Did her desire to kill stretch to her late husband? She had a temper, but so did Elita. Maybe Lonnie simply liked his women feisty.

"Let's get out of here," I muttered to Helen. I called Flipper to get out of the water.

"Good plan," she said, "before Sylvia tries to drag us into communicating with the dead."

I put my shoes back on and squelched to my bedroom, Flipper stopping to shake water off his fur several times before catching up.

I pulled off my clothes and had a quick shower to wash off the smell of chlorine.

When I came back in the bedroom, Helen and Flipper were on my bed, and Lonnie was drifting around the room.

"Which one of your angry wives should we focus on for your murder?" I asked him as I towel dried my hair.

"I thought it was cold in here. Lonnie's here?" Helen asked.

I nodded. "Did you notice that Elita and Chelsea were fighting over the house, not the fact they missed their late husband?"

Lonnie's pout was so exaggerated, I couldn't help but smile.

"They've got their priorities right," she said. "They need to look after themselves."

"Who do you think we should focus on for your murder?" I asked Lonnie. "Everyone is interested in the house and the gold."

"It's got to be one of the wives," Helen said. "It must be so frustrating having to share a house when they hate each other."

"I blame Lonnie for ramping up their hatred of each other," I said. "It wasn't the smartest move to split the house between them and expect them to get along."

Lonnie frowned.

"What did you expect would happen?" I asked him. "You dumped Elita for Chelsea and expected it to be all sunshine and roses between them?"

"Chelsea's determined not to let go of this house," Helen said. "Maybe she thinks the gold is hidden here and needs time to look around."

"Ignatius brought up the missing gold just now. Maybe we should still focus on him. And he did do his creepy goon impression on me in the limousine."

Lonnie drifted over to me, concern on his face.

"Don't worry. Your charming brother didn't do anything. He simply suggested he would if I didn't play by the rules."

"We should keep Carson in mind, as well," Helen said. "He could be feeling betrayed because he never got his fair share of the gold."

"Betrayed enough to make Lonnie pay." I tugged my fingers through my damp hair.

"If the motive wasn't hatred or revenge, it could be about love," Helen said.

"Michael and Elita?" I sat on the edge of the bed.

She let out a sigh. "Love and hate. There are so many good reasons to want Lonnie dead."

Lonnie scowled and shook his head at Helen.

"He doesn't like that idea." I looked at Lonnie. "I can't help it if you weren't a lovable guy when you were alive."

That comment only made his scowl worse before he blinked out of sight.

I pulled out some clean, dry clothes and headed back to the bathroom. "Let's start with Ignatius, and see what we can discover about him."

Helen poked her head around the bathroom door. "That man gives me the chills for all the wrong reasons."

I nodded as I smoothed down my hair. "Me too. Let's get him out of the way. If he wasn't the killer, we have plenty of other options to keep us busy." And that was a problem. We were surrounded by criminals and running out of time.

Chapter 18

The next day, the house was quiet when I got up. I ate breakfast with Helen and Flipper in a comfortable silence before going to the study, which was empty.

I was just completing a sneaky look through some private files when Elita breezed through the door. "Good morning. We have lots to do today, Lorna."

"I've already made a start," I said as I slid the file drawer shut.

"You're such a good girl." She patted my arm. "And thank you for helping me yesterday. Chelsea is proving to be a problem."

"It must be tricky having to share your home with her."

"Tricky is one way of putting it." Elita sank into the chair behind her desk. "I wonder if the easiest thing would be to move out and find my own place, but this has been my home for years. We moved here after Lonnie's business affairs were wound up."

"Business affairs being gold robbery?"

Elita gave me a shrewd look but didn't comment.

My eyes strayed to the desk where the gold was concealed. "Do you think Lonnie would ever have come clean about what he did?"

"He was torn about that," she said. "Part of him knew stealing was wrong, but he could see the good he'd be able to do with so much money. And although he didn't tell me what happened to the gold, I know he had some melted. I overheard him talking to someone about it and planning mold designs to pour the gold into. It makes it easier to transport and sell on."

"Maybe it was taken out of the country. If I was trying to hide so much gold, that's what I'd do."

Elita smiled. "We'll make a criminal mastermind of you yet. And he might have done that. That was one good thing about my Lonnie. If he ever did anything naughty, he never told me about it. He didn't like to think I'd get in trouble if the worst happened. He was so thoughtful like that."

It amazed me how Elita was happy to skim over the fact Lonnie had been unfaithful to her and left her for someone else. That was hardly thoughtful.

She looked at her watch. "I haven't had any breakfast yet. Why don't you head to the kitchen and see if they can sort out some brunch? You'd be welcome to join me."

"Brunch sounds lovely." I left Elita in the study along with Flipper, who was dozing on the rug by the fireplace.

As I walked past a window on my way to the kitchen, I spotted Ignatius in the garden. He was strolling toward the pond, a plastic bag in one hand.

Before I could convince myself it was a stupid thing to do, I headed out the door and followed him.

He slowed, and before I had a chance to hide, turned and looked in my direction.

Ignatius's thick dark eyebrows rose. "Shouldn't you be working?"

"I'm taking a break." I walked closer to the pond. "How about you?"

Ignatius gave me a lopsided smile. "I came out here to feed the fish." He shoved his hand into the bag and scattered a handful of pellets into the water. "We keep Koi Carp. They could probably take a finger off if you let them. They get big."

"I didn't know Koi had teeth." I peered into the water and saw a bright orange head appear, its mouth open as it grabbed the pellets of food.

Ignatius chuckled and continued throwing food into the water. "I like fish. I go shark fishing when we're in Hawaii. Nothing beats taming a wild beast. I always eat what I kill. Have you ever eaten shark?"

I repressed a shudder. "I prefer seeing them in the sea where they belong."

He shrugged. "The flesh can be gristly, but I do enjoy the hunt."

I cleared my throat. "About our recent car journey."

Ignatius held up a hand. "It's best we don't mention that to anyone. It was important you know where you stand. I've seen staff come and go who haven't understood their place in this household. And you've got such a pretty face. I'd hate for that to disappear."

I unpicked several threats in those words. "I definitely don't want my face to disappear, or any other part of me. I'm not going to cause problems." Although, I'd like to cause problems for Ignatius. The man had a serious attitude.

"You know, there are also piranha in here." Ignatius gestured to the water.

"Don't they eat the Koi Carp?" I looked into the murky depths of the pond.

"The carp can hold their own." Ignatius grabbed my arms and spun me so my back was facing the pond.

"What are you doing?" My fingers dug into his arms, determined not to get another drenching.

"Just seeing how easy you are to scare." Ignatius smirked. "And making sure you don't get any silly ideas to go poking your nose in where it's not wanted."

I glanced at the water, half expecting to see a dozen hungry piranha glaring back at me. All I saw was the giant, slow-moving orange body of a carp.

"Do you want to take a closer look at the fish?" he asked. "They really are beautiful."

"I can see them well enough from here." I aimed a kick at Ignatius's shin, but he avoided it and laughed.

"I'm only joking with you." He let go, and I dodged out of his way before he changed his mind and threw me into the pond.

"You have a very different sense of humor to me." I glared at him and rubbed my arms where his fingers had dug into my flesh.

"I like my women to find the fun in life," Ignatius said. "It's one reason I've always liked Elita. She could always find a reason to laugh, even when Lonnie wasn't treating her right."

"Elita has been kind to me," I said. "Lonnie should have stayed with her. I bet she was good for him. Do you know why they split?"

"Because he's a fool," Ignatius said, screwing the bag up in his fist. "And he thought he could get the edge over me by taking her away."

"You and Elita were together?"

He shot me a glare but then nodded. "I met her at the Candy Club in London. She wasn't even eighteen at the time and lied about her age so she could start earning money. There she was, working the room and getting all the hopeless idiots who fell for her charms to buy expensive bottles of champagne. She caught my eye the second I walked in. She had on a bright red corset and a long black skirt with a slit up her thigh. It wasn't so much her beauty that captured my attention, but her laugh. I don't hear her laugh much anymore."

"Is that why you wouldn't help Elita when she was fighting with Chelsea?" I asked. "You're still angry with her because she didn't choose you?"

Ignatius shrugged. "It was a long time ago. We were just kids."

"First love lingers," I said.

"I never said anything about love."

Despite his denial, I could tell Elita meant more to Ignatius than he was letting on. And if Lonnie took her away from him, that could leave the desire for revenge.

"Chelsea and Elita are a problem these days," Ignatius said. "Lonnie dropped us all in it by leaving them half the house each. They fight over it constantly. I can't see that changing."

"Your suggestion they each buy a house would solve the problem. It was a good suggestion."

"What would have been good was if they'd both drowned in the swimming pool," Ignatius said. "Then they wouldn't constantly go on about wanting the gold."

I scrubbed my nose. It had been Ignatius who'd brought up the gold yesterday. "It must keep you awake at night wondering what Lonnie did with it."

"Knowing how soft Lonnie had become, it wouldn't surprise me to learn he melted it down and gave it away," Ignatius said. "He lost his edge before he died, ever since deciding to retire the family here."

"And you don't approve of being here?"

"Changing where you live doesn't change your nature." He shot me a wry smile. "There I go, getting all poetic on you. You'll accuse me of being a philosopher if I don't keep my mouth shut about my messed up family."

I doubted that, but this conversation was useful. Ignatius still had a thing for Elita and a grudge against his brother. Perfect motives for wanting Lonnie dead.

"Are you going to keep searching for the gold?" I asked.

"I'm not sure where else to look." Ignatius gestured to the garden. "The only place I haven't turned upside down is out here. Lonnie barely spent any time in the garden. Well, he liked to play with his toy tank sometimes. He had a real thing for collecting military vehicles. It was the one thing he never liked anyone helping with. It was his weird little hobby. And it would be a rookie mistake anyway, burying it. Buried things are hard to uncover. I've lost count of the number of guns I've had to write off after hiding them in a hole. Some of them were my favorites. It's hard to find a good gun these days."

I opened my mouth but then snapped it shut. I didn't need to know about Ignatius and what he did with his guns. It couldn't be anything good.

"I should leave you to your fish." I stepped away. "I need to get back to work."

Ignatius's phone rang in his pocket, and he took it out. "Run along then. And just remember, if you stick to the rules, we'll get along fine."

I hurried away from the pond, glad to be leaving Ignatius's intimidating presence. He had the gangster model down to a tee. He was intimidating, and made me even more certain he'd killed Lonnie.

Now, all I needed was some proof.

Chapter 19

I'd made it less than fifty steps from Ignatius when a muscular arm shot out from behind a broad oak tree and grabbed me.

My heart leaped in my chest as I dug my fingernails into the arm wrapped around my waist. I kicked out, making contact with the shinbone of whoever was holding me.

I wriggled out of my attacker's grip and spun around. Michael stood in front of me, massaging his shinbone, a frown on his stubbled face.

I glared at him. "What do you think you're doing?"

"I wanted to talk to you."

"So talk! There's no need to grab me and whisk me into the bushes. I had no idea it was you."

"I didn't want anybody to see us." Michael straightened and shook his leg. "You've got quite a kick on you."

"I'll kick you again if you don't tell me what's going on." I folded my arms over my chest. "And you shouldn't be skulking around out here. People will think you're up to no good."

Michael pointed over his shoulder. I glanced over to see Sylvia asleep in her wheelchair. "I wasn't doing anything dubious. I've been taking Sylvia around the gardens when she nodded off. I thought she'd appreciate some shade while she slept. I was waiting here until she woke. Then I saw you talking with Ignatius and thought I'd better warn you about him."

"Why do I need to be careful of Ignatius?" I didn't need to ask that question, having almost been thrown into a pond by him. It didn't take a genius to figure out Ignatius wasn't to be trusted, but I was interested in what Michael thought of him.

"There's something off about him," Michael said, keeping his voice low. "I don't trust him around Elita."

"You think Ignatius is trying to hurt Elita?"

Michael's jaw muscles twitched. "He's sending her gifts and trying to get on her good side. I know what he wants with her. He's never going to worm his way into Elita's bed."

"Is Elita interested in Ignatius?" I asked. "Wouldn't it be a bit strange, her marrying her ex-husband's brother?"

"She can't stand the guy," he said. "She'd never consider marrying him, or doing anything with him."

"Elita doesn't mind having him around the house, though."

Michael shrugged. "Ignatius is family. You have to put up with them, no matter how stupid they are."

"You don't want to put up with him," I said. "Has this got something to do with your feelings for Elita?"

Michael's head shot up and his eyes widened. "What do you know?"

"You're fond of her. I saw the way you helped her after she fell into the swimming pool. And... I might have seen you on a date with her."

"Have you been following Elita?" Michael took a step toward me, anger flaring in his eyes.

"Not for a second," I said, "but you're not great at hiding the fact you like her. And she's a nice lady. I understand why you're interested in her."

Michael scuffed his feet on the ground and his shoulders slumped. "She's a lovely lady. Too good for me."

"There's nothing wrong with you," I said. Well, I was a bit concerned he was more into using his fists than his words, but as I'd gotten to know Michael, I realized he was simply shy, which made him appear stand-offish.

"Have you been seeing each other long?"

"I've always liked Elita." Michael's cheeks glowed. "I never said anything or did anything about it when she was married to Lonnie. And I never thought she'd look twice at me. Then Lonnie left her for Chelsea, and Elita was heartbroken. I made sure I was always around so she had somebody to talk to. We got to know each other, and well, things just happened."

"She made a move on you?"

"I was happy about it," Michael said, a small smile sliding across his face. "I remember the day well. I'd taken her out shopping, and was standing around with half a dozen bags waiting for her to finish in the last store. When Elita came out, she handed me a tiny brown bag and kissed me. I wasn't bothered about what was inside the bag. Her kiss was the best present I'd ever gotten. Since then, we've been together."

"Does the family know?"

"Of course not," he said. "The hired muscle doesn't get to be with the lady of the house."

"Technically, that's now Chelsea," I said. "Elita's a free woman. Since Lonnie divorced her, surely she's able to date anyone she likes."

"Providing the family approves of the match," Michael said. "And they won't approve of our relationship. I don't mind keeping it a secret, so long as I get to see Elita happy."

I looked over to check Sylvia was still asleep. "What about Lonnie? Perhaps he figured out the two of you were seeing each other and didn't like it."

"I don't think he'd have liked it," Michael said. "Even though he was no longer with Elita, he didn't want anyone else to have her. That wasn't fair. He threw aside someone as lovely as Elita, then refused to let her find happiness with another man."

I took a deep breath and stared directly at him. "That's a good motive for murder."

Michael blinked several times. "Murder! Who do you think I murdered?"

"Lonnie! I'd understand if you got frustrated about keeping your relationship with Elita a secret. If you thought Lonnie had figured out you were dating, you might have felt you needed to get rid of him before he forced Elita to give you up."

Michael shook his head. "There's no way I'd hurt Lonnie. Why would you even think that? His death was an accident."

"So everyone's been led to believe," I said. "But his death has left the way clear for a lot of people to get their hands on what he's been hiding."

"You think someone killed Lonnie for the gold?"

I nodded. "It doesn't add up the way Lonnie died. He always used the radio in the bathroom. He'd have known where to place it safely. And people in this house would have known his routine, known about his love for singing loudly to music while in the bath. It would have been easy to sneak in and throw the radio into the water."

Michael's jaw dropped. "I can't believe that. No one mentioned any foul play when it came to Lonnie. Everyone said it was an accident."

"With Lonnie gone, the way is clear for the family to hunt for the gold, without having to hide what they're doing."

"They are obsessed with finding it." Michael grunted and shook his head. "But to kill Lonnie. No way."

"Lonnie's death also left the way clear for you to pursue Elita without him looking on with disapproval," I said. "Did he find out about the relationship and threaten you if you didn't end things?"

Michael frowned at me. "That never happened. Lonnie was my idol. He taught me everything I know. I'll always be grateful to him for that. And he introduced me to Elita. The first time we met, I was a teenager. Elita's older than me, but she was the most beautiful woman I'd ever seen and has a laugh that makes my toes curl. I couldn't believe it when she took an interest in me. I'm the luckiest man alive, although I don't deserve to be."

"If you make Elita happy, then you deserve her. You deserve to be with her," I said. "Lonnie didn't treat Elita well when they were married. It's right she gets a happy ending."

"He was always messing around behind her back," Michael said. "I know part of the reason he did it was because he wanted children and refused to believe he was firing blanks. We all knew the truth, but no one had the guts to tell him. When I think of all the nights I had to stand outside Elita's bedroom and hear her sobbing herself to sleep because Lonnie didn't come home..."

"And that made you angry enough to kill him?"

"No! I was loyal to Lonnie. I doubt I'd be alive if it weren't for him," Michael said. "He had his faults, we all do, but I'd never do anything to harm Lonnie. If you know for sure he was murdered, though, I'll help you get whoever killed him. That can't go unpunished."

Loyalty ran deep in Michael and I found myself warming to him as he revealed his feelings for Elita. It must have been frustrating to stand by and do nothing when he cared for her so deeply. To do so proved he was loyal to Lonnie.

"I don't know for sure who's involved in Lonnie's murder," I said. "You said to be careful around Ignatius. Do you think he would ever harm Lonnie?"

"They had their moments when they'd beat on each other." Michael scratched his stubble. "Ignatius always loved violence and is always looking for a fight, looking to wind people up enough so they snap and give him a reason to attack. Sometimes, he doesn't even bother doing that. He simply picks a fight and goes to town on the person he's taken a dislike to."

I swallowed my nerves as I recalled my alone time with Ignatius in the limousine. I'd been lucky to get away with just a warning.

"You get used to violence being in this line of work," Michael said. "But some of the things I've seen Ignatius do still make my stomach cramp."

Ignatius had the same effect on me. "I understand Lonnie was going to use some of the gold to set up a charity."

Michael smiled. "Lonnie was really into his charity. He talked about it all the time. I wish there had been something like that for me when I was growing up. Things could have been different."

"Other people weren't supportive of getting the charity going?" I said. "All the trouble taken to steal the gold and then to learn it would be invested in something that would never make money. That's got to sting."

Michael shrugged. "Lonnie realized the stealing and violence weren't great. He knew it was time to start giving back. He wanted to be seen as a rogue with a heart of gold."

"If only people could find that gold," I said. "You've no idea where it's hidden?"

"Lonnie didn't share that information with anyone," Michael said. "It drove Ignatius mad that he wouldn't divulge the location."

"No one involved with stealing the gold got to keep any of it?" That would add quite a few names to the suspect list if that was the case.

"People got paid," Michael said. "And Lonnie did something with one of the gold bars and gave away some expensive jewelry. The rest vanished. Lonnie said when the heat died down, he'd start turning the gold into money and handing it out. We just had to bide our time."

"So those involved understood it would be a few years before anyone got their hands on significant amounts of money?"

"That's right," he said. "It's always that way when you steal a lot of cash or assets. You don't start showing off your newfound wealth, or you'll end up behind bars quicker than a world class whippet in a ferret chasing race."

"It's been years since the gold was stolen," I said. "Isn't it time to start distributing the wealth?"

"That's what Ignatius has been saying." Michael stared at me and his gaze hardened. "You really think Ignatius killed Lonnie?"

I raised my hand. "I don't have any proof Ignatius was involved, but he seems like a solid suspect."

"That wouldn't surprise me," Michael said. "He always wanted to be famous like some of the big name gangsters. He hated the need to be so sneaky and not show off about some of the crimes the family has been involved in. That's the way you get put in prison. Keep your mouth shut and everything is fine. You follow the rules and no one gets hurt. Lonnie taught me that."

Those words sounded eerily like the warning Ignatius had given me. Stick to the rules. It was all about following the family code.

"Michael's right." Sylvia lifted her head and stared straight at me. "My boys are like darkness and light, one a demon and the other an angel. If anyone killed Lonnie, it was his brother."

Chapter 20

I walked over to Sylvia, who looked surprisingly alert, considering she was supposed to have been asleep.

"Michael's right to warn you to be careful about my remaining boy," Sylvia said. "I'll love Ignatius until my last breath, but he has a dangerous side. I'd hoped him being around Lonnie would help to change that, make him less twisted in his desires, but I don't think Lonnie had much impact."

It sounded like Sylvia had been listening to my whole conversation with Michael. "And you think Ignatius killed Lonnie?"

"Why don't you ask him yourself?" Sylvia said, her gaze sliding over my shoulder.

I felt the touch of cold fingers on my arm and turned to see Lonnie.

"Don't overexert yourself, Mrs. Cornell," Michael said. "You start seeing things when you haven't had enough rest."

"I start seeing things because they're really here," Sylvia said. "And Lorna can see Lonnie as well. Don't start pointing your big finger at me and accusing me of being a crazy old woman."

"I'd never do that." Michael shot me a worried look. "You can't see Lonnie, though, can you?"

Sylvia nodded at me. "Tell him the truth. He's hardly going to fire you."

I chewed on my bottom lip. "He might tell Elita if I say I see ghosts."

"Can you?" Michael took a step back and his gaze shot around the trees. "You're saying Lonnie's here?"

Lonnie drifted to Michael and pressed a hand to his face.

Michael shivered and took another step away.

"Don't be scared," I said, "but Lonnie is standing in front of you. And Sylvia's right; he is still here. We can both see him."

Michael swallowed loudly. "Does Lonnie know who killed him? If he tells me, I'll sort them out."

"You'll do no such thing," Sylvia said. "You're a good boy. I don't want you getting into trouble over this. We will deal with it, but not at your expense."

"I don't mind doing time for Lonnie," Michael said. "I'd do anything for him."

Lonnie touched Michael's arm and smiled, making Michael shiver and go pale.

"He knows that," I said. "But he wouldn't want you going to prison. We'll find out who killed Lonnie and make sure he goes away for a long time."

"Or she," Sylvia said. "Don't underestimate the women in this household."

"I thought you were convinced that Ignatius killed Lonnie," I said.

"I'm as sure as I can be Lonnie was killed by his brother," Sylvia said. "But I also don't like Chelsea. She might have put Ignatius up to it. Whoever's involved, I've got people on the inside of most prisons. They'll be happy to make sure Lonnie's death doesn't go unpunished."

I stared at her. "Even if it was Ignatius who killed Lonnie?"

"Of course." Sylvia's eyes narrowed. "Nobody hurts my boys and gets away with it. Ignatius needs to learn a lesson."

"We're getting ahead of ourselves." I could see Sylvia was getting worked up.

"We need a confession from Ignatius." Sylvia slapped her hands on the arms of her wheelchair. "Lorna, have you any experience wearing a wire?"

A trickle of fear ran through me. "No! And I'm not keen on wearing a wire and trying to get Ignatius to confess to murder. What if he discovered what I was doing? He's already tried to throw me in the pond today."

"Maybe a wire is risky," Sylvia said. "At least get him to confess to what he's done and make sure there are family members listening. They won't believe my ramblings. After all, I'm a crazy old woman who sees the dead. They won't believe you, either. This family sticks together. An accusation of murder won't hold up if it doesn't come straight out of Ignatius's mouth."

Michael rubbed his forehead and leaned against an oak tree. "I'm not feeling so good."

I rushed over and caught hold of him as he began to sway. "Take a few deep breaths. It's a lot to take in, finding out Lonnie was killed and his ghost is still here."

"No kidding." Michael sucked in air. "The killer will be found and punished. I swear that to Lonnie."

Lonnie patted Michael on the shoulder.

"Why don't you take Sylvia back to the house?" I said to Michael. "You both need a rest after this."

Michael ran a hand down his pale face. "Yeah. Good idea."

"I'm fine," Sylvia said. "I spend my whole time being told I need to rest, or take this pill, or do this type of exercise. I'm ready to figure out who killed my Lonnie and give them a knuckle sandwich."

"And we'll do that," I said. "But we don't want to arouse suspicion, and we need to be sure who the killer is."

Sylvia sighed. "This would have been finished by now if I wasn't stuck in this chair. We'd have sorted out justice, and Lonnie would be avenged."

I walked next to Michael as he pushed Sylvia's wheelchair toward the house. "We can make sure the killer gets what they deserve without having to kneecap them."

Sylvia tutted. "As if I'd do anything as basic as knee capping. Now, talk to me about water boarding and we're onto something."

I decided not to pursue that gruesome topic of conversation. We walked along in silence until we reached the house. I left Michael and Sylvia in the hallway, with Sylvia trying to convince Michael she wanted to go out onto the terrace and take a swim.

I hurried to the study, long overdue getting back to work with Elita. She must be wondering where I was with our brunch.

Slowing my pace, I tilted my head, hearing a man and woman talking quietly. I snuck toward the door the voices were drifting out of and poked my head inside.

Ignatius was in the room with his arms wrapped around Chelsea! Was everyone having a secret affair in this house?

"We have to finish the job, babe," Chelsea said.

"It's almost done. Then we're getting out of here," Ignatius said.

"We can finally be alone," she said. "No more sneaking around in this stuffy house."

"I thought you loved this house."

"I'll pretend to love it for as long as it annoys Elita," Chelsea said. "That woman only has to look at me and I want to punch her in the face."

Ignatius gave a low chuckle. "That's my sister-in-law you're talking about."

"That doesn't mean I don't want to punch her," Chelsea said. "I can't believe you used to have a thing for her."

Ignatius's shoulders tensed. "That was a long time ago. You're all the woman I need now."

"Just me and the gold," Chelsea said. "That's the deal. We find the gold, we cover our tracks, and we get away from here."

He kissed Chelsea. "That's the plan. I was thinking Hawaii might be a good place to start."

"I want to go to Mexico," Chelsea said. "Drink tequila and dance on the table tops all night."

"That's a sight I look forward to seeing."

I slipped away from the door, my heart thudding in my chest. This was the proof I needed. The bimbo wife and the evil brother must have killed Lonnie together.

A loud wolf whistle pierced the silence in the hallway, and I ducked.

I'd only taken a few steps away from the room where Ignatius and Chelsea were plotting their evil scheme. If they caught me, I'd be busted.

"Coo-eee! Lorna! Get out here." I cringed as Sylvia shouted my name.

I turned and peered along the hallway, seeing Sylvia sitting in her wheelchair on the terrace.

I was gesturing at her to be quiet when the door opened and Ignatius looked out.

"What's going on?" He glared at me.

"I was going to see what Sylvia needs." I backed away a few steps, but Ignatius lunged at me. He dragged me into the room before I had a chance to squeak out a protest, slammed the door, and clicked the lock into place.

"Is there something you need?" I licked my lips as I stared into Ignatius's fury-filled eyes.

"What were you doing in the hallway?"

Chelsea bustled over, her high red heels clicking on the wooden floorboards. "What's going on, babe? What's Lorna doing here?"

"We've got an eavesdropper," Ignatius said.

"I wasn't listening." I hoped my bottom lip wasn't trembling.

"The door was open," Ignatius said. "You must have heard us."

I looked at Chelsea, and she peered back at me with a confused expression on her face. "I might have heard you talking. I don't know what it was about."

Ignatius crowded my personal space, forcing me against the door. "I can always tell when you're lying, remember?"

I cursed my inability to hide my emotions.

"It's not a problem," Chelsea said. "She's on my side. I'm paying her off. Lorna works for me."

"Does she?" Ignatius kept his glare pinned to me. He was so close I could smell his cologne and the coffee on his breath. "What information has she been passing to you?"

"Nothing yet," Chelsea said, "but she's only been here a few days. You can trust Lorna." She pulled a wad of money from her cleavage and handed it to me. "He can trust you, can't he?"

"Of course, I can be trusted." I waved away the bundle of money.

"Can you be trusted not to tell anyone what you've heard?" Ignatius asked.

"Babe, calm down." Chelsea placed a hand on Ignatius's arm. "Lorna doesn't mean any harm. And even if she did hear us, what good would it do her? She knows you're loyal to the family."

"I am loyal," Ignatius said. "That doesn't mean I can allow people to start causing trouble for me. I get the feeling Miss Shadow is going to cause me a lot of trouble."

"Why would I do that?" I fought the panic surging up my throat. "If you've not done anything wrong, there's nothing I can tell people about."

"You saw me with Chelsea."

"Chelsea's a free woman," I said.

"She was my brother's wife."

"Lonnie's dead," I said. "Chelsea's not doing anything wrong if she wants to be with you."

"That's right." Chelsea smiled at me. "We're doing nothing wrong."

I nodded at her. Although why Chelsea wanted to be with Ignatius was a question a therapist would need to unpick over many sessions.

Ignatius shook his head. "We sort this out the old-fashioned way. I can't have someone running about with information that'll cause me problems, especially not someone so new to this family. Elita might trust you, and Chelsea's daft enough to think she can bribe you, but I know what you're like. You've been poking your nose around ever since you got here. It needs to end."

"What are you going to do to her?" Chelsea asked.

"Get Frankie to bring the van round the front," Ignatius said. "Lorna and I are going for a ride."

"I don't want to go for a ride." My mouth went dry. "I can't go anywhere. Elita's expecting me back any second. She'll come looking for me."

"She'll understand that you had to leave suddenly," Ignatius said. "We've lost staff before who couldn't handle the heat. The fact you disappear and leave your belongings behind won't come as any surprise. And you're easy to replace."

"No, I'm not," I said.

A fist thudded against the door. "What's going on in there?"

I let out a relieved sigh. It was Sylvia, and she sounded mad.

"Nothing to worry about, Mom," Ignatius said.

"I saw you with Lorna. Let me in." Sylvia started thumping on the door again, making a surprisingly loud noise for such a small person.

"This isn't your business," Ignatius said, his tone hardening. "Isn't it time for your nap? You must be overdue some medication, as well."

"I'm not a baby. I don't need to take a nap." Sylvia kept thumping. "I'll start screaming for help if you don't unlock the door this instant."

Ignatius growled in my face, then yanked me away from the door before flipping the lock and pulling it open.

Reggie leaped off Sylvia's lap and launched himself at Ignatius. He seized hold of a finger and clung onto like it was his favorite bone.

Ignatius yelped and grabbed the dog. "What's he doing?"

"Protecting Lorna." Sylvia peered into the room. "You alright, girl?"

My hands were shaking and I clasped them behind my back. "I am now."

"Get this crazy mutt off me!" Ignatius was tugging on Reggie's collar, but he held on fast. Blood dripped on the floor where his teeth had sunk into Ignatius's flesh.

"He'll let go when I tell him to," Sylvia said.

Ignatius staggered backward and tripped over a chair, landing with a thump on the ground.

Reggie jumped up and down on his chest as he continued to bite his finger, an amazingly deep growl coming from such a tiny dog.

The scrabbling of claws on wood made me turn my head. Flipper bounded along the hallway, jumped straight over Sylvia's wheelchair, and landed at Ignatius's feet. His hackles raised, and he grabbed one of Ignatius's pant legs and started shaking it.

"Get these animals off me!" Ignatius yelled.

Chelsea hovered around him, her hands flailing in the air as she tried to shoo the dogs away. "What should I do, babe?"

"Grab this little runt," Ignatius said. "He's trying to work his teeth through to the bone."

"You leave Reggie where he is," Sylvia said. "He's under my instruction and is allowed to do whatever he likes."

I watched as the two dogs attacked Ignatius. Although Flipper had hold of his clothing, he wasn't biting him.

"Mom, get these dogs off me," Ignatius said, his tone turning pleading. "I wasn't doing anything wrong."

Sylvia watched as Reggie continued to chew on Ignatius's finger. "Down boy."

Reggie gave a final shake of Ignatius's hand and let go. He made an angry sounding yip and peed on Ignatius's jacket before trotting back to Sylvia.

Reggie would be getting a giant bone as a thank you from me.

"That dog's a menace." Ignatius gripped his injured finger to his chest.

I beckoned Flipper away, and he came to my side and sat at my feet. He had a sorrowful look on his face as if he felt bad because he'd not been around to help me. I'd make sure he got a bone, as well. After all, I was the one who left him sleeping when I went on my investigations.

"It's no more than you deserved," Sylvia said. "Now, tell me what you were doing to Lorna?"

"We weren't doing anything," Chelsea said. "We were just worried—"

Sylvia held her hand up. "Not from you. I want to hear what my son was doing. Lorna's a valuable member of staff. I will not have her mistreated."

"I wasn't treating her badly." Ignatius's shoulders slumped as if he knew he'd been defeated. "You don't even know her."

"I know you. And you were up to no good." Sylvia beckoned me toward her.

"I was just giving her a bit of a scare," Ignatius said. "She's nosy and keeps asking questions, trying to get into our business."

"That's not acceptable. No scaring the staff," Sylvia said. "How many times do I have to tell you?"

"It's not fair. You always take away the things I enjoy." Ignatius was sounding more like a spoiled child by the second.

"Lorna is off-limits," Sylvia said. "She's under my protection now."

That seemed to clinch it for Ignatius. He gave a single nod. "I won't touch her."

I let out a breath I'd been holding, happy to hear those words. Now, for the difficult bit. Getting a confession out of Ignatius. "From what I heard of your conversation with Chelsea, it sounds like you were up to no good."

Ignatius glared at me. "You don't know what you're talking about."

Chelsea frowned. "Lorna! You're supposed to be on our side."

"I'm not on anyone's side." I glanced at Sylvia.

"Spit it out, girl," Sylvia said. "Get him to tell you everything."

Ignatius glowered at his mom. "What's going on?"

I took a deep breath. "We think you killed Lonnie."

Chapter 21

Ignatius's hands fell to his sides. "I'd never kill my brother."

"You were just talking about finishing the job," I said. "You murdered Lonnie so you can get your hands on his gold and his wife."

"I wouldn't do that." Ignatius glanced at Chelsea. "Fine. I was having a bit of fun with Chelsea. It's nothing serious."

"What are you talking about?" Chelsea jammed her hands on her hips. "It's serious. You love me!"

He shrugged. "You're fun to be around, but I was never serious about you."

"Of course you are!" Her eyes narrowed. "We're leaving this horrible place and going away together."

"*I'm* leaving," Ignatius said. "There's not a chance in hell that we're going anywhere together."

Chelsea spluttered out some unintelligible words, her face growing red.

Ignatius shrugged again and looked at me. "I had my problems with Lonnie, but we settled them like men. I'd never wimp out and throw a radio in the bath to get rid of him. Lonnie wouldn't want to die like that. He wanted to be remembered for what he was, a successful gangster.

Someone who beat the police, got what he wanted, and didn't care who got hurt along the way."

"That's not my Lonnie," Sylvia said. "He was turning over a new leaf, making some good changes in his life. Although, not all of them were good." Her gaze slid to Chelsea, who stood with her mouth open, still glaring at Ignatius.

"I don't understand what's going on," she said. "What about the gold? What about our new life in Mexico?"

"Sweetheart, you can go to Mexico if you want to," Ignatius said. "Sell your half of this house to Elita and you'll be set for life. You can get a little house, as much tequila as you like, and life will be perfect."

"That wasn't the plan," Chelsea said through gritted teeth. "You said you wanted to make Elita pay."

"I wanted to make her pay for leaving me for Lonnie," Ignatius said. "I don't want her to leave this house, though. You, however, were a temporary addition to this family. Lonnie regretted marrying you almost as soon as he put the ring on your finger."

"And he only did that because you pretended you were pregnant," Sylvia said. "You knew how badly Lonnie wanted a child, so you tricked him."

A sob shot out of Chelsea. "I didn't trick him. I thought I was pregnant."

"Only until you were married," Sylvia said.

"I made a mistake."

"One you're going to regret," Ignatius said.

Chelsea's bottom lip jutted out. "We have to be together. We have a plan."

"I have my plan. It's different from yours." Ignatius turned away from Chelsea. "Why don't you pack your bag? I can book you a flight out of this country, leaving tonight."

"I'm not leaving without my money," Chelsea said. "I put up with Lonnie and pretended to like you and your grubby, greasy hands. I'm owed because of that."

"You'll get what's due to you." Ignatius's tone made me think Chelsea would be lucky to get away with her life.

She also seemed to recognize the tone. She backed away and hurried to the door. "You're going to pay for this."

"Do your worst," Ignatius said.

Chelsea gave an angry squeak before shoving past me and out into the hallway. She stomped up the stairs and slammed a door.

"Now that annoyance has gone," Ignatius said as he removed his dog pee smelling jacket, "why don't you tell me what you know about Lonnie's death? Why do you think I killed him?"

"You have the most to gain," I said. "Lonnie refused to tell you what he'd done with the gold. You hated him for that."

Ignatius looked at his mom. "You believe this crazy theory?"

"I know something happened to Lonnie," Sylvia said. "I see him around the house every day. He wouldn't be here if he'd simply had an accident."

"And you see him too?" Ignatius looked straight at me.

Sylvia waved her hand at me. "Don't be shy around him, girl."

I still wasn't used to people believing I could see ghosts. "I've seen Lonnie's ghost. He's convinced me his death wasn't an accident."

"He's pointing the finger at me?"

"Not exactly," I said. "Lonnie's not sure who killed him."

"Which means you've got no proof," Ignatius said. "I had nothing to do with it."

I wasn't going to believe that. "You must want to get your hands on the gold."

"Of course," he said. "Half the criminal underworld wants the gold. Are you going to add them to your list of suspects as well?"

I bit my lip. Annoyingly, what Ignatius said was true. It wasn't just this family who'd like to get the stolen goodies.

"Don't keep things from us, boy," Sylvia said. "Tell Lorna everything. I trust her."

Ignatius examined his damaged finger and then leaned against the back of a chair. "I'll admit, we wanted different things when it came to the gold. I wanted to ship it overseas, liquidate what we could, and invest in property. We could hold tight on the investments for a few years, and when the police lost interest, sell the investments and reap the rewards. Lonnie had gotten all goody-two-shoes and wanted to give the gold away and set up that ridiculous charity."

"Which was a noble thing to do," Sylvia said. "Your brother had my full support."

"But the gold was also mine. Lonnie didn't get to spend it how he wanted."

"You would have gotten your share," Sylvia said. "Lonnie hoped that, when you saw the good his charity was doing, you'd invest your money into it."

"That would never happen," Ignatius said. "I was thinking about going away. I planned to buy a few properties and spend my time in the sun. I hear there's a growing market for extortion in Belize."

"And leave the family?" Sylvia asked.

"You'd do alright without me," Ignatius said.

"We need someone to head up this family."

"I was never good at any of that." Ignatius looked at his chewed finger. "That was Lonnie's thing."

"You need to step up and do your bit now he's gone," Sylvia said. "Learn to be a better man. Lonnie was our public face. His warm handshake and easy manner meant others joined us and kept quiet when we needed them to. He's not here anymore, and we need somebody to keep doing that."

"I thought the Cornells had retired from a life of crime?" I asked.

Sylvia frowned at me. "We still have our moments."

Ignatius looked at the floor. "That's not who I am, Mom."

"Then learn to be," Sylvia said. "You've got it in you. You can't abandon us for hot sand and bimbos in bikinis. You'd get bored."

"I wouldn't get too bored." Ignatius grinned at his mom.

"I can still spank you if I have to," she said.

Ignatius raised his hands in mock surrender. "Spare me the slipper."

"Do you know where the gold is?" I asked Ignatius. "You have to have some idea, or you wouldn't have killed Lonnie."

"For the last time, I didn't kill Lonnie!" he said. "I have no idea where the gold is."

"Where were you going to get the money to leave?" I asked. "Without the gold, what would you live on?"

"I wasn't dependent on Lonnie for money." Ignatius looked at his fingernails. "I make my own cash."

"You were," Sylvia said. "You're terrible with money. It goes on the horses or women."

Ignatius frowned. "If you must know, I was going to get Chelsea to sell her share of this house and take the money. I want the gold, but I've looked everywhere for it. It's vanished. Lonnie has taken that secret to his grave."

I shared a look with Sylvia. That wasn't true. With Lonnie's ghost still in the house, there was a way to find the gold. I just needed to convince Lonnie to show me where the rest was hidden and then figure out just how involved Ignatius was in Lonnie's death.

This mystery was almost solved.

Chapter 22

"Then Sylvia intervened and saved me. With a little help from Reggie and Flipper." I sat opposite Helen in my bedroom, having just finished updating her about my unpleasant encounter with Ignatius and Chelsea.

Helen shook her head. "That's quite a day you've had."

"Sylvia was amazing," I said. "She really put Ignatius in his place. You can tell who's in charge in this family. It's not the men."

"How were things left?" Helen asked.

"Ignatius muttered something about having business to attend to and skulked away. We're no closer to finding the gold, though, or getting proof to show who killed Lonnie." I ran my hand along Flipper's back as he snoozed on the bed. "If Sylvia hadn't been there, the outcome would have been very different."

"Should we get Zach and Gunner to come rescue us?" Helen asked. "The Cornells aren't messing around when it comes to this gold."

I was tempted to give up. "Let's give it twenty-four hours. If we're no closer to figuring out who killed Lonnie, I think we should go."

"You're still convinced it was Ignatius who killed Lonnie?"

"I'm still leaning toward him, despite his protests. He's got so much to gain from Lonnie's death."

"There's always Carson," Helen said. "I wandered into a spare bedroom yesterday and caught him pulling up the carpet. He said he was looking for a clean shirt! I bet he was on the hunt for gold."

"I've barely seen Carson since I've been here," I said. "He keeps below the radar. It won't do any harm to check him out." And by investigating him, I could keep away from Ignatius and his poorly veiled threats to get rid of me.

"It's getting late. Carson's probably in his own apartment having dinner," Helen said. "Which is what we should be doing. I've been dealing with the laundry and darning all day. Some of the stuff I've been pulling out of the laundry hampers has been odd, to say the least."

"What have you found?"

"Well, I was in Chelsea's room. She'd left a note saying she needed some items altered. I decided to sort through her laundry as well and make sure I wasn't missing anything. I pulled out a set of handcuffs covered in pink fur!"

"Ignatius and Chelsea have kinky tastes."

"I dropped them right back in the laundry hamper." Helen shuddered.

"So long as they enjoyed themselves, I guess it's not our business."

Her nose wrinkled. "Chelsea should keep her toys somewhere private."

I grinned. "Let's go see what Carson's doing. It won't surprise me if he's involved with Lonnie's murder, as well. Everyone in this family has trouble keeping on the straight and narrow."

Helen followed me out of my bedroom, along with Flipper, who'd remained glued to my side ever since he'd discovered me being hassled by Ignatius and Chelsea. I think it was his way of apologizing for not being there to protect me.

He didn't need to worry. With Sylvia and Reggie on my side, I had great backup.

We left the house through the back door, keeping to the late evening shadows as we hurried to Carson's apartment, which sat close to the main house.

I hit two cold spots as we walked, and stopped so fast Helen ran into me.

"What's wrong?" she asked.

"Do you feel that?" I held my hands out, the tips of my fingers going numb.

"The chill?"

"Yes. I keep walking through them when I'm in the garden."

"Is it a ghost?"

"If it is they never show up." I rubbed my arms. "Maybe all the criminal vibes are just setting me on edge."

"Or being so close to Carson is making you feel weird." Helen gestured me over to the apartment. It was a large single-story structure, covered in trailing roses and ivy. It didn't suit his tough guy persona. I'd expected minimalist sleek structure, all chrome and glass, with flashy cars sitting out front. Maybe Sylvia had decorated it for him.

One of the windows was open, and I stopped by it and had a look inside. There were half a dozen men sitting around a table playing cards, all dressed in similar dark suits. The room was fitted out with pale green sofas and a widescreen TV. Country and western music played in the background.

"Anything interesting?" Helen whispered.

"Just a poker game by the looks of it," I said.

"No master plan to steal the gold pinned on the wall?"

"If only it were that easy."

We listened by the window for five minutes, but all I could hear was laughter and the occasional crude joke.

"We should try to get inside," Helen said. "There could be something incriminating in there. And if we don't find anything, we can rule out Carson and focus on the others."

I didn't like the idea of being discovered searching through Carson's things, but Helen had a point. I couldn't avoid investigating him just because he was a bit of a slime bag.

The sound of something being scraped over gravel made me turn my head. I spotted Sylvia pushing her wheelchair along the pathway away from the house.

I squinted as something glinted on her lap. Wedged on the handlebars of her wheelchair was a black duffel bag.

I took a few steps away from Carson's apartment, and my mouth fell open. "I think Sylvia's got a gold bar on her lap!"

"What? Are you sure it's not Reggie?" Helen asked. "She takes that dog everywhere."

I pointed at Sylvia as she continued to push herself away from the house. "I've never seen a dog look like that."

Helen's eyes widened. "She must have known where the gold was all the time."

"And she's stealing it." I continued to watch Sylvia's slow progress.

"Does that mean Sylvia killed Lonnie so she can have the gold for herself?"

"We need to find out." Sylvia had been lying. She knew all about the gold. She knew where it was hidden and was making off with it. This whole time, she'd fooled me into thinking Ignatius was Lonnie's killer.

I ran across the grass with Helen and Flipper, determined to stop Sylvia.

Sylvia's head whipped around as she heard us approaching, and her eyes narrowed.

"No, you don't." I grabbed the handles of her wheelchair. "Where are you going? And why have you got a gold bar on your lap?"

"I'm keeping it safe." her hands covered the bar of gold.

I yanked the duffel bag off the handlebars and opened it to discover three more gold bars. "You were trying to escape?"

"I was doing no such thing." Sylvia let out a sigh. "I need to protect the gold. Ignatius is insistent he has it. I can't risk that. He only needs one gold bar in order to escape. Then I'll never see him again."

"You know where all the gold is?" I asked.

She lifted her chin. "What if I do?"

"Did you kill Lonnie to get your hands on it?" Helen asked.

Sylvia shook her head. "Hush! Keep your voice down. I'd do no such thing. I loved my boy."

"Perhaps you love the gold more," I said.

"You're going to accuse me of killing Lonnie?" Sylvia spun her wheelchair around and glared at me. "First, you accuse Ignatius and now me. I'm beginning to think you don't know what you're doing."

She was right there. "You certainly do, though. Sneaking off at night with the stolen goods. That's not going to look good to the police."

"Don't get them involved," Sylvia said. "They're not welcome here."

Reggie's head poked out of the purse on Sylvia's lap and he growled.

Flipper stepped in front of me and matched Reggie's growls, sounding twice as fierce.

A gust of cold wind blew my hair over my face. As I pushed it back, I spotted Lonnie's ghost behind Sylvia's wheelchair.

She also sensed his presence. She twisted her head and looked straight at her dead son. "Don't get angry. I'm not stealing your gold. I'm keeping it safe."

Lonnie scratched his chin, and his confused gaze went from his mother to me.

I held my hands up. "I have no clue what's going on." I'd never figured Sylvia as the killer. How could she have wheeled into Lonnie's bathroom without him hearing her? She must have had help.

"This is family gold," Sylvia said. "I'm not stealing it. I knew Lonnie had a secret place in his desk where he kept a few gold bars for emergency situations. When Ignatius began talking about leaving, I had to move the gold somewhere safe. I can't have him abandoning this family."

The front door of Carson's apartment opened, and his head popped out. "What's going on out here? All the yelling is disturbing our card game."

"Don't let him see the gold!" Sylvia placed Reggie over the gold in her lap. "He's worse than Ignatius, always sniffing around looking for it."

Carson strolled over, a beer bottle in one hand and some cards in the other. "Is everything okay, Sylvia?"

"Everything's fine. Go back to your card game."

"What have you got there?" Carson came closer and peered into Sylvia's lap, ignoring the menacing growls coming from Reggie. His eyes widened, and he dropped the bottle of beer.

"This isn't your business, Carson." Sylvia pressed her hands together and glared up at him.

"Of course it's my business," he said. "Where did you get the gold bar?"

"Lonnie gave it to me before he died," she said. "It's the only one I know about."

Carson's gaze went to the bag in my hand. "I suppose Lonnie gave you some gold as well?" He made a grab for the bag, but I swung it out of his reach, my muscles straining under the weight of the gold inside.

Two of the men who'd been playing cards with Carson emerged from the apartment and strolled over. "What's happening?"

"Get over here, AJ and Max. We've found some gold," Carson said.

The men exchanged a glance and strode over.

Lonnie spun around Sylvia, panic in his eyes. He looked at me as if he expected me to help.

"This is your mess," I whispered to him.

"The old lady's been hiding it all along," Carson said, as AJ and Max stopped by his side.

"Show some respect," Sylvia said. "You still work for this family."

"Only until I get my hands on that." Carson pointed at the gold. "You've saved me the trouble of tearing this place down brick by brick until I find it."

"You killed Lonnie to get the gold?" The question popped out before I could stop myself.

Lonnie stopped flying around and focused on Carson.

"Nah! Lonnie's death was an accident. You keep out of this." Carson gestured to AJ and Max. "Get the gold, boys."

They strode toward Sylvia, but I blocked their way, not feeling as brave as I looked. "Stay away from her. She's just an old lady."

Sylvia snorted. "I'll whip those two. Don't worry about me."

Part of me wanted to run as fast as I could, but there was no way I could leave Sylvia with these thugs. They wouldn't simply take the gold and vanish. They'd want to get rid of all witnesses.

"Make this easy on yourself," Carson said. "Hand over what you've got there and we'll go. I only want what I'm owed."

"You said we'd get it all," one of the men said.

"Keep quiet, AJ," Carson snapped. "What's here will set us up for life."

"The boss won't be happy about that," Max said.

"Shut your mouth," Carson hissed. "This amount of gold will see us right. We can take off and forget about the others."

"You double-crossed us." Steel ran through Sylvia's words. "You're working for someone else. Someone who is after our gold."

Lonnie floated next to Sylvia, anger on his face as he glared at Carson.

Carson smirked. "Of course I'm working for somebody else. Lonnie held out on us all. No matter how many times I tried to persuade him to let me know where the gold was stashed, he wouldn't budge. We all knew he was going to waste it on some dumb charity. He should have divided it among the people who were loyal to him."

"He would have seen you right in the end," Sylvia said.

"Which is why you were running off into the night with it," I said to her.

"Don't be so foolish. I wasn't going anywhere," Sylvia said.

"It's our gold," Carson said. "Hand it over."

AJ grabbed at the gold on Sylvia's lap, but received a bite from Reggie for his efforts. He backed off and pulled a gun from his waistband.

Helen squeaked and backed away.

"There's no need for violence," I said, my gaze glued to the gun. "This can be settled over a nice cup of tea and a chat. I'm sure we can come to a suitable compromise."

"The time for talking is over," Carson said. "We want what's owed us."

"Lonnie wouldn't want you to do this," I said.

Lonnie nodded and jabbed a finger at Carson.

Carson pulled out his own gun and swung it toward me. "How do you know about Lonnie?"

I swallowed, my heart thudding. "I know you murdered him."

Carson shrugged. "What if I did? I had to get rid of anyone who showed too much interest in the gold, or wanted to do something dumb with it."

I looked around the garden and felt light-headed. The cold spots! Had I really been walking through ghosts this whole time? "How many people have you killed?"

"I lost count. They didn't learn, though. They just keep on coming."

I swallowed. The ghosts I'd experienced had been trying to show me where Carson buried them. No wonder this place weirded me out the second I'd arrived. It was a murder hotspot.

"Have you been working undercover for Lonnie?" Carson asked.

My eyes widened. "No! I'm really just a personal assistant. I never met Lonnie. Why did you kill him?"

Carson adjusted his grip on the gun. "He'd gone soft and was an embarrassment to this family. I did everyone a favor by getting rid of him. The Cornell name won't now be ruined by Lonnie becoming a do-gooder, and the gold can be shared out to people who'll use it properly."

"I'm guessing you're not going to invest your gold in any good causes," I said.

"I've got a few investments I'll make. Nothing like Lonnie had planned."

I held the bag of gold tightly, determined not to give it to Carson. "This is only a tiny amount of gold. Lonnie hid it in his desk."

Sylvia's head whipped around. "You knew about that hiding place too?"

"Lonnie showed me," I said. "Well, I sort of found it by accident, so he had no choice but to show me."

"Before he died?" Carson asked, his fingers tightening on the gun. "I knew it! You can't be as straight as you appear. Lonnie's had you working for him, getting information. How long have you been spying on me? I knew Lonnie was suspicious of me asking questions about the gold. That was another reason I had to get rid of him."

"No! Nothing like that," I said. "I promise you. I'm as straight as I look."

"Lorna sees ghosts, the same as me," Sylvia said, shooting a pointed look at Lonnie.

AJ laughed. "Ghosts! Is she being serious?"

"Ignore her. She's a mad old woman. She's always going on about seeing the dead." Carson focused his attention back on me. "If you knew Lonnie before he died, and he told you about that hiding place, perhaps he told you where the rest of the gold is."

"I didn't know Lonnie when he was alive," I said, my knees beginning to shake.

Flipper and Reggie growled in unison as Carson took a step toward me.

"Keep the mutts out of this," Carson said. "I'm happy to waste a bullet on them."

"Don't you dare." Helen stepped in front of the dogs.

I shot her a grateful look for defending Flipper and Reggie.

"I enjoy a good dare," Carson said. "It keeps things lively. Which one will be first? The little runt or the wolf with the freaky blue eyes?"

Flipper jumped at Carson at the same time as Helen kicked him in the knee.

Carson roared with anger as Lonnie joined in the fight, latching onto his wrist and making Carson drop his gun.

Lonnie spun away and vanished/.

Reggie jumped off Sylvia's lap and sat on the gun, a pleased expression on his furry face.

Sylvia rammed her chair into Max's legs just as I threw myself at AJ.

AJ gave a surprised grunt as he dropped his gun and hit the ground, my knee making contact between his legs as I landed on top of him.

Flipper ran over to help and growled in AJ's face.

I ground my knee into AJ's groin. "If you value your crown jewels, you won't move." I wasn't sure if my threat was effective, but the fact Flipper was baring his teeth an inch from AJ's throat meant he didn't even blink.

I looked over to see Max squashed under Sylvia's wheelchair. My heart pounded as I spotted Carson had shoved Helen to the ground and was scrabbling for the gun Reggie concealed with his furry butt.

"Lonnie!" I yelled.

Lonnie appeared, but he wasn't alone. Five more ghosts materialized, their angry glares fixed on Carson, and shot straight through him.

His victims had come back for some well-timed revenge.

Carson froze to the spot, and his eyes widened as the ghosts hit him. "Wait! What just happened?"

"Are you okay?" I shouted to Helen.

Helen rolled over and frowned at the grass stain on her dress. "I'll be fine."

"Don't worry. Lonnie and his friends are on the case," I said. "Carson doesn't know what hit him."

Lonnie and his ghostly sidekicks wheeled in a circle and charged toward Carson again, grabbing the back of his jacket and yanking him across the grass.

Carson's arms flailed as he tried to keep his balance. He was followed by an angry looking Reggie, who nipped at Carson's ankles whenever he got within range.

AJ moved underneath me, and I pressed my knee in harder, making him grunt and stop squirming.

"We called the police!" Chelsea and Elita ran out of the house, clutching each other's hands. "We saw what happened. Help's on the way."

I let out a sigh, surprised to see the women working together.

Now, all I needed to do was keep AJ pinned to the ground while Lonnie and his buddies kept Carson busy, and Sylvia continued to squash Max with her wheelchair, and everything would be fine.

Chapter 23

My heartbeat felt like it was back to normal as the police loaded Carson in the back of their car. He was the last person to be taken away.

The police had arrived quickly after Chelsea and Elita alerted them to what was happening outside the house. We now had several armed police striding around as the evidence was collected and statements were taken.

Elita and Chelsea stood side by side talking to the police. Their newfound bond was holding. It might not be for long, but at least, they'd stopped fighting to help us.

Michael hovered nearby, Elita's ever faithful companion. I hoped things worked out between them. He was a sweet guy and Elita deserved happiness.

Sylvia sat by the door to the main house with Reggie on her lap and Ignatius by her side. Every time he said something she told him to be quiet. She must want to keep him off the police's radar in the hope they'd think the gold theft was all Lonnie's doing. He'd be lucky. Ignatius deserved prison time after everything he'd put me through.

And it was more by luck than expertise that we'd stopped Carson and his gang from taking the gold. If the rest of his gang had come out of the apartment to see what was going on, we'd be dead.

I looked at Flipper, who sat by my side, taking in the scene. "I don't think we'll do that again anytime soon."

He stood and paced away from me before coming back, his attention flitting from me to the driveway.

I expected to see Lonnie appear, but after the fight, he'd vanished and had yet to return. His ghost friends were also missing, but something was bothering Flipper.

Helen walked out of the house, a tray in her hand, which was full of mugs of tea.

I let out a relieved sigh as Zach's Land Rover shot along the driveway and stopped outside the house. That's what Flipper must have sensed.

Zach jumped out and ran over to me, closely followed by Jessie. He pulled me against his chest before stepping back, his worried gaze running over me.

"I'm fine." I'd called him as soon as the police had arrived.

Gunner got out of the Land Rover and strolled over. Despite trying to appear nonchalant, I could see a tightness around his eyes as he focused on Helen.

"Everybody is fine," I said.

"I ruined my dress," Helen said. "It'll take ages to get these grass stains out."

"You're only fine because you were lucky," Zach said. "You should never have taken this job. And you should never have agreed to go digging around and trying to get proof the Cornells stole that gold." He shot an angry look at Gunner.

"Finding the gold wasn't all that hard," I said. "Discovering who killed Lonnie was a bit trickier. There were so many possibilities."

"Who did kill him?" Gunner asked.

"Carson Rosso," I said. "He's been double crossing the family and figuring out a way he can get his hands on the gold. And he's been killing off people interested in the gold. You'll find some interesting things in the garden when you start digging." That was something I didn't want to stick around for.

"Carson's been killing his rivals?" Zach asked.

I nodded. "At least five people are dead. All thanks to Carson's greed."

"It doesn't surprise me. He's as slippery as a sand eel," Gunner said. "We've got an open file on him, and are investigating his involvement in several serious offences."

"You can add robbery and murder to that list," I said.

"Already on there," Gunner said. "You're sure you're both okay?" Again, his gaze shot to Helen.

"Stop flapping around us," Helen said. "Have a mug of tea."

Gunner smiled at her and took a mug. "It seems like nothing ruffles your feathers."

"Please tell me you aren't going to keep working here," Zach said. "I've hardly slept worrying about you."

I looked at Helen. "I think our time as undercover agents is over."

"Suits me," Helen said. "We can come help at the house, instead."

Gunner groaned. "I don't want you getting under my feet and trying to convince me to paint every room pink."

"Don't be an idiot," Helen said. "My favorite color isn't pink."

"What is it?"

"It's lavender," Helen said.

Gunner groaned again. "That's even worse. And I suppose you're going to try to persuade me to have scented candles in every room, as well?"

"I'll have them in my bedroom," Helen said. "That's somewhere you're never getting into."

"Don't be so sure of that." Gunner grinned.

Helen tutted and passed around the rest of the tea.

"I think it's a good idea," Zach said. "You can come and work on the house. It'll be great having you there. We can start putting in the furniture, and the kitchen is well on the way to being finished."

I looked at the Cornell house. Every light was on and the warm amber glow blazed into the night, chasing away the darkness. "This job was going to pay for the furniture. We should try to find something else. Otherwise, we won't be able to move in so quickly."

"We can sit on old boxes until we have enough money for the fancy stuff," Gunner said.

"You might be able to do that," Helen said. "I'm not sitting around on dusty old boxes."

"I'll let you sit on my lap if you sweet talk me enough," Gunner said.

Helen shook her head, but she was suppressing a smile.

I looked over her shoulder. Lonnie was drifting backward and forward. "Give me a minute. I've got a bit of unfinished business to sort out."

Zach reluctantly let me go, and I walked over to Lonnie.

He drifted across the lawn, and I followed him all the way to his collection of military vehicles.

"I guess you're going to miss all of this," I said as he stopped by a tank.

Lonnie shrugged and then nodded.

"At least you know what happened to you," I said. "It wasn't anyone in your family who killed you."

Lonnie nodded again.

"And your ghostly helpers?" I looked around. "They can show themselves if they want to."

Lonnie gestured with his hand and five more ghosts appeared on either side of him. They all had on smart suits and slicked back hair.

"Thank you. Hope you all find some peace now Carson's been arrested. The police will find out where he buried you and make sure you all get a decent burial and your families know what happened."

The ghosts all nodded, and that tense, dark vibe I'd been dogged by since I'd arrived faded. All they wanted was resolution for their murders. Now they had it.

I leaned against the tank. "So, that only leaves the rest of the gold. Any chance you're going to tell me where it is?"

Lonnie smiled and winked.

"Is that a yes or a no way in hell am I ever going to find out what you did with the gold?"

Lonnie's smile widened, and he pointed at the tank I was leaning against.

"I can't believe you spent all the money on buying these old bits of tin."

He shook his head and tapped his knuckles against the tank.

I copied his movement and banged the side of the tank. It didn't make the metallic sound I expected. In fact, it sounded much denser, as if the tank was full of something.

"Don't tell me you've hidden the gold inside the tank?" I asked, half-joking.

Lonnie nodded.

"Why didn't anyone look inside and see the gold bars?"

Lonnie's grin only widened.

I scrambled on top of the tank and twisted the hatch open. Inside, there was nothing but blackness. There was no gold.

"You're messing with me." I slid off the tank and back to the ground.

Lonnie shook his head again and knocked the side of the tank.

I took a few steps back as an idea formed. Elita had mentioned overhearing Lonnie was getting molds made to use for the melted gold. Could he have hidden the gold in plain sight and simply changed the shape of it?

"Lorna, what are you doing?" Zach approached with Gunner, Helen, and the dogs.

"Your friend Lonnie was quite a collector." Gunner's gaze ran over the military vehicles. "He's got Scimitar tanks and Jackals here, three Coyote tactical vehicles, and a Lynx helicopter. How did he get one of those?"

"I have a hunch the missing gold is inside these vehicles," I said.

"Not possible," Gunner said. "I checked the records. Everywhere was searched."

"Well, it's not so much as inside them as on them."

"Huh! Where does your hunch come from?" Gunner's gaze roved over the vehicles.

"Call it an insider tip," I said. "Can you find a hammer to bash the side of this tank? I think we're going to find something interesting when we do."

Lonnie drifted backward and forward, the other ghosts watching with interest as Gunner went to the Land Rover and returned with a hammer.

I could see Lonnie was anxious about us finding the gold. He must have mixed feelings about giving up its location, but the police wouldn't stop hounding his family until they'd gotten what they wanted, especially now some of the gold bars had been discovered.

I took the hammer from Gunner.

"You won't do much damage with that," Gunner said. "These things are made to survive direct missile strikes."

"I don't want to blow it up, but it'll be easier to damage than you think. Let's see what we discover." I took a deep breath and smashed the hammer into the side of the tank. Nothing happened other than my muscles protesting at their unexpected use. I did it several more times. Suddenly, a piece of the green tank chipped off and flew over our heads. Underneath shone the yellow gleam of gold.

Helen laughed. "You've got to be kidding me! Lonnie melted the gold and covered these vehicles with it?"

"He must have," I said. "Ignatius said he never liked anyone to touch them. Now, we know why. He hid the gold right under people's noses." I looked around at the thirty or so tanks, armored personnel carriers, and helicopters.

Gunner let out a low whistle. "The guy was clever. Melt down the gold, reshape it into something else, give it an acrylic cover, and paint it. Lorna, you're a genius."

"It was Lonnie, not me."

"Right." Gunner ran a hand through his dark hair. "I'd better call this in. The team isn't going to believe it. And to be honest, neither can I. I knew the two of you were good at solving mysteries. This is something else."

"That doesn't mean they're going to do it again," Zach said. "Not ever. No more working for criminal families. No more going undercover for Gunner."

"We will if we want to." Helen folded her arms over her chest. "I'll work where I like."

"You'll always want to help me, beautiful," Gunner said to Helen. "That's what friends are for."

Helen blinked at Gunner and her cheeks grew pink. "Yes. I guess we are friends."

The look on her face was priceless. I hoped they'd get together soon. Otherwise, I'd have to install a cold shower in Helen's room.

Zach wrapped an arm around my waist and pulled me toward him. "So, your ghost is happy?"

I looked over to see Lonnie and his ghost friends fading away, a sad smile on his face. "He's content now he knows who killed him. Carson will go to prison for a long time. Lonnie might not be happy his gold is going back to its rightful owners, but showing us its location was the right thing to do."

We both turned and looked as the sound of splintering acrylic filled the air. Gunner was smashing the side of a helicopter. Helen stood next to him, directing him as to which bit to hit next.

I shook my head as they began to bicker over the best way to break through to the gold, and snuggled into Zach's arms.

Lonnie's murder had been solved, the gold had been found, and a ghost could be at peace.

This was the strangest job I'd ever had. But even with the regular threats to my life over the last week, I wouldn't change a single thing we'd just achieved.

"After this, you deserve a holiday," Zach said.

"Don't we have a house to finish building?" I smiled at the thought of living with Zach.

"The house can wait."

I looked up at him. "I don't want it to. No more living apart. Let's finish the house, then we can think about a holiday."

"Just the two of us?" he asked.

"You want to leave Jessie and Flipper behind?"

The dogs raced past an armored personnel carrier.

"They always come with us," Zach said. "It might be time to let Gunner and Helen sort themselves out while we're not around."

"That sounds perfect." I watched as Gunner discovered more hidden gold, and let out a sigh.

Our next job would be a quiet one. No mystery to solve, no ghosts, and definitely no guns. I shook my head. Who was I kidding? I'd get bored with quiet. I wouldn't have my life any other way.

***

Want to find out what's next for Lorna and Flipper? Get Ghostly Waves and meet the new ghosts in Lorna's life.

Read on to learn more.

Ghostly Waves

A watery death. A ghost with four legs and a tail. And a heap of suspects.

Lorna Shadow, Helen, and Flipper have just begun to enjoy life in their new house with Zach, Jessie the dog, and Gunner, when an exciting job offer arrives. They head off to work in the glorious county of Cornwall to enjoy their new jobs by the sea.

Yet when they arrive, they find an exhausted widow, a sneaky assistant, a mistress, and a mysterious death. And when there's a mystery, there's often a ghost.

When Lorna learns that the death of Blake Carlisle wasn't accidental, she's determined to discover what happened to him. His murder deserves to be solved so he can be at rest. But was his affair with a younger woman the reason for his murder? Or did a relative want him out of the way to lay claim to the family fortune?

There's a killer hiding in broad daylight and Lorna must find the truth. Bring on the sleuthing, cups of tea, treats, and even a glass of wine this time.

With trouble brewing at home and a possible marriage proposal on the cards (but for who?), Lorna has a lot of distractions. And it's not helped by Helen's not-so-secret relationship with Gunner and poor Flipper getting sick every time he boards the family yacht.

If she fails in her sleuthing task, a killer could go free and a ghost will never find peace.

Enjoy Ghostly Waves in paperback or e-book.

Complete series list

Ghostly Manners
Ghostly Secrets
Ghostly Games
Ghostly Affairs
Ghostly Business
Ghostly Rules
Ghostly Waves
Ghostly Play
Ghostly Proposal
Ghostly Vows
Ghostly Fright
Ghostly Hunt
Ghostly Surprises

About the Author

K.E. O'Connor (Karen) is the author of the adorably fun Lorna Shadow cozy ghost mystery series, the wickedly funny Crypt Witch paranormal mystery series, the Magical Misfits Mysteries featuring a sassy cat with a bundle of twisty puzzles to solve, the slightly darker Witch Haven paranormal mystery series featuring four troubled witches and their wonderful furry (feathered and web-slinging companions), and the whimsical, delicious Holly Holmes cozy culinary mysteries.

Stay in touch with the fun mysteries:
Newsletter: www.subscribepage.com/cozymysteries
Website: www.keoconnor.com
Facebook: www.facebook.com/keoconnorauthor

www.ingramcontent.com/pod-product-compliance
Lightning Source LLC
Chambersburg PA
CBHW020807190726
48285CB00006B/2190